HEAVEN AROUND THE CORNER

KU-613-237

BY
BETTY NEELS

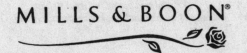

MILLS & BOON®

*First published in Great Britain 1981 by Mills & Boon Limited
This edition 1996
Harlequin Mills & Boon Limited,
Eton House, 18-24 Paradise Road, Richmond, Surrey, TW9 1SR*

© Betty Neels 1981

ISBN 0 263 79893 3

*Set in Times Roman 12 on 12½ pt by
Rowland Phototypesetting Limited
Bury St Edmunds, Suffolk*

73-9610-44988

*Printed and bound in Great Britain
by Caledonian International Book Manufacturing Ltd, Glasgow*

Dear Reader,

Looking back over the years, I find it hard to realise that twenty-six of them have gone by since I wrote my first book—*Sister Peters in Amsterdam*. It wasn't until I started writing about her that I found that once I had started writing, nothing was going to make me stop—and at that time I had no intention of sending it to a publisher. It was my daughter who urged me to try my luck.

I shall never forget the thrill of having my first book accepted. A thrill I still get each time a new story is accepted. Writing to me is such a pleasure, and seeing a story unfolding on my old typewriter is like watching a film and wondering how it will end. Happily of course.

To have so many of my books re-published is such a delightful thing to happen and I can only hope that those who read them will share my pleasure in seeing them on the bookshelves again. . .and enjoy reading them.

Betty Neels

Back by Popular Demand

A collector's edition of favourite titles from one of the world's best-loved romance authors. Mills & Boon are proud to bring back these sought after titles and present them as one cherished collection.

BETTY NEELS: COLLECTOR'S EDITION

CHAPTER ONE

THE September sun, shining from an early morning sky, cast its impartial light on the narrow crowded streets, the smoke-grimed houses, several quite beautiful churches and the ugly bulk of the Royal Southern Hospital, giving a glow to its red bricks and a sparkle to its many narrow windows. It was a splendid example of mid-Victorian architecture, crowned with cupolas and a highly ornamental balustrade and rendered even more hideous by reason of the iron fire escapes protruding from each wing. And inside it was even uglier, for here the sun was unable to reach all its staircases and passages, so that the dark brown paintwork and distempered walls tended to cast a damper on anyone passing through them.

But the girl going down the stairs two at a time noticed none of these things. Her neat head with its crown of light brown hair was full of excited thoughts. She had passed her State finals; she was a fully trained nurse at last—the world was her oyster. She was determined on that, despite the Principal Nursing Officer's gracious speech as she was handed the fateful envelope. There was a place for her at the Royal Southern, that lady told her; Night Staff Nurse on the surgical wing and the prospect of a Sister's post very shortly, and there was no need for Nurse Evans to decide at once. . .

But Louisa Evans had already decided instantly; she was going to leave, not only the hospital, but if possible, England too, although she prudently forbore from saying so at the time. At the end of the day, when she went off duty, she was going to write her resignation and hand it in and then she would go home for her two days off and tell her stepmother. She checked her headlong flight for a second, dreading that, but it was something which had to be done, and she had made up her mind to that weeks ago when she sat her exams.

She went along a narrow corridor, up another flight of stairs, across a wide landing and through the swing doors leading to Women's Surgical. Just for the moment the future wasn't important, only the delicious prospect of telling Sister and the nurses on the ward that she was an SRN.

And she had no need to tell anyone. Sister, coming out of her office, took one look at Louisa's happy face and said: 'You've passed—congratulations, but of course I knew that you would.' And after that the news spread like wildfire, with the patients, only too glad to have something to talk about, telling each other, nodding their heads and saying, with hindsight, that of course Nurse Evans had been bound to pass, she was such a good nurse. And as for Louisa, she floated up and down the ward, doing her work with her usual efficiency while a tiny bit of her mind pondered the problems of what she should do and where she should go.

A problem solved sooner than she had expected: She had been to her midday dinner—a noisy meal she shared with friends who had reached her exalted position too—and she was back on the ward, changing Mrs Griffin's dressing, when that lady asked her what she intended doing.

Louisa, aware of how news, false as well as true, travelled with the speed of light round the hospital, said cautiously that she hadn't quite made up her mind, and rolling the lady carefully back into a sitting position, rearranged her pillows, smoothed the counterpane and prepared to depart with her dressing tray.

'Well, don't go for a minute, Nurse,' begged Mrs Griffin. 'Listen to this: ''Trained nurse urgently required for lady patient travelling to Norway in a month's time for an indefinite stay. Good salary and expenses paid.'' What do you think of that?' She folded the *Telegraph* and handed it to Louisa, who read it carefully, and having an excellent memory, noted the telephone number. 'It sounds fun,' she observed cheerfully. 'Someone'll be lucky.' She drew back the curtains and with a parting nod raced off down the ward to clear the tray and get on with the next dressing. But before she did that, she jotted down the telephone number on to the hem of her apron.

She went off duty at five o'clock, composed her letter of resignation and handed it in for delivery to the office and then went to telephone from the box in the entrance hall. There was no one about; she could see the porter on duty, sitting with his feet up, sipping tea during his brief break. All her friends were already in the Nurses' Home, getting dressed for the party they were all going to later on that evening. She dialled the number.

The voice at the other end asked her to wait a moment and after a few seconds another voice spoke. Louisa had had all the afternoon to rehearse what she was going to say and she was listened to without interruption. When she had finished, the voice, a woman's, high and somehow breathless, said: 'I have interviewed several nurses already, but none of them suit me. Come and

see me tomorrow morning about eleven
o'clock.'

'I'm on duty until the early afternoon. . .'

'Oh, well, the afternoon then, about three
o'clock. I'm at the Connaught Hotel, and ask
for Miss Savage.'

Louisa put the receiver down slowly. Miss
Savage had sounded petulant; she wondered
what complaint the lady suffered from, but
the only way was to go and see her and find
out. Even if she were offered the job, she
need not accept it.

She started to stroll along the passage to
the small door which opened into the Nurses'
Home. On the other hand, if she were offered
the job it would be like the answer to a
prayer—she had been longing to leave the
hospital for some months now, not because
she was unhappy there—on the contrary, she
had enjoyed every minute of the three years
she had spent within its walls—but because
her stepmother, living not too far away, had
been able to keep tabs on her for that time,
knowing that she had set her heart on training
as a nurse and wasn't likely to leave the Royal
Southern and was therefore unlikely to
escape. But now she could do just that. . .
She quickened her steps, intent on not being
late for the party.

They had all decided to dress rather
grandly for the occasion. Louisa, burrowing

around in her cupboard, wasted a good deal of time deciding whether the pale blue crêpe would look better than the sage green silk jersey. On second thoughts she didn't like either of them, she had had them too long although she hadn't worn them all that much. She chose the green and rushed off to find an empty bathroom.

Half an hour later she was dressed and ready—a rather small girl and a little too thin, with a face which wasn't quite pretty although her eyes, large and hazel and fringed with long curling lashes, redeemed it from plainness. Her hair, long and fine and silky, she had fastened back with a silver clasp because there hadn't been time to do anything more elaborate. Presently her friends trooped in and they all went into the hospital to the residents' room where the housemen and some of the students had laid on a buffet supper. The room was packed already, with everyone talking at once and quite a few dancing to a barely heard tape recorder. Louisa, popular with everyone because she was ready to lend an ear to anyone who wanted it, was quickly absorbed into a group of young housemen, all of whom looked upon her as a sisterly type to whom they could confide their troubled but fleeting love affairs, for she never told them how silly they were but listened to their outpourings, giving sympathy but never advice. For a girl of twenty-two she had a wise head on her shoulders, albeit a rather shy one. Her stepmother had taken care that she had had very little chance of making friends while she was at school and when she left, until she had succeeded at last in her ambition to train as a nurse; she had been kept too busy to do more than meet the people Mrs Evans approved of, most of them elderly or at least middle-aged, so that she still retained the feeling of not quite belonging among the young people at the hospital, certainly she had shied away from any of the young men of her acquaintance who had hinted at anything more serious than a kiss, and they, once they had laughed about her among themselves, but kindly, had taken to treating her like a sister.

She joined the dancers presently and except for short pauses for food and drink, didn't lack for partners for the rest of the evening. The party broke up around midnight and they all went their several ways, yawning their heads off and grumbling at the prospect of getting up at half past six the next morning. All the same, they made a pot of tea and crowded into Louisa's room to drink it and discuss the party, so that it was an hour later before she went finally to bed, too tired to give a thought about the next day.

She dressed carefully for the interview in

a thin wool suit with a slim skirt and a short loose jacket, it was a pretty grey and she wore a silk shirt in navy to go with it; a suitable outfit, she considered, making her look older than her years, which she considered might be a good thing.

The hotel looked grand and she went inside feeling a great deal less calm than she looked, but the reception clerk was pleasant and friendly and she was led to the lift and taken several floors up and along a thickly carpeted corridor until the porter tapped on a door and opened it for her.

Louisa had expected to be interviewed in one of the reception rooms of the hotel; presumably her patient was confined to her room. And a very handsome room it was too, splendidly furnished with wide french windows and a balcony beyond—and quite empty. She walked into the centre of the room and waited, and presently a door opened and a chambermaid beckoned her. It was an equally luxurious room, this time a bedroom, and sitting up in the wide bed was, she presumed, Miss Savage.

Miss Savage wasn't at all what Louisa had expected her to be. She had entertained the vague idea that the lady would be elderly and frail: the woman in the bed was still young—in her thirties and pretty with it. She had golden hair cut in a fringe and hanging in a gentle curve on either side of her face, her make-up was exquisite and she was wrapped in soft pink, all frills and lace.

She stared at Louisa for what seemed a long time and then said surprisingly: 'Well, at least you're young.' She nodded to a chair. 'Sit down—you realise that we may be in Norway for some time if you come?'

Louisa said, 'Yes,' and added: 'Will you tell me something of your illness? I couldn't possibly decide until I know more about that—and you must want to know a good deal more about me.'

Miss Savage smiled slowly. 'Actually I think you'll do very well. You're young, aren't you, and haven't been trained long.'

'I'm twenty-two and I became a State Registered Nurse yesterday. I've not travelled at all. . .'

'Nor met many people? From the country, are you?'

'My home is in Kent.'

'You won't mind leaving it?'

'No, Miss Savage.'

The woman picked up a mirror and idly examined her face. 'I've got a liver complaint,' she observed. 'My doctor tells me that I have a blocked duct, whatever that is, I'm not bedridden but I get off days and he insists that if I go to Norway I should have a nurse with me.' She shot a glance at Louisa.

'My brother works there—he builds bridges—somewhere in the north, but I've arranged to take a flat in Bergen for a month or so.'

'You have treatment, Miss Savage?'

'Doctor Miles looks after me, he'll recommend a doctor to treat me.'

'Yes, of course. But if you can get about, will you require a full-time nurse?'

Miss Savage frowned. 'Certainly I shall!' She sounded petulant. 'I often have bad nights—I suffer from insomnia; you'll have more than enough to do.' She put the mirror down and began to buff her nails. 'I intend to go in a little over three weeks—you'll be free then?' She glanced up for a moment. 'You'll be paid whatever is the correct rate.'

Louisa sat quietly. It seemed a strange kind of interview, no talk of references or duties. She had the impression that Miss Savage wasn't in the least interested in her as a person. The job was just what she had hoped for, but there was something about this girl that she didn't like. That she was spoilt and liked her own way didn't worry Louisa overmuch, but there was something else that she couldn't quite put her finger on. On the other hand, if she didn't take what seemed like a heaven-sent chance, she might have to stay in England.

'I accept the job, Miss Savage,' she said

at length. 'You will want references, of
course, and I should like a letter from you
confirming it. Perhaps you'll let me know
details of the journey and my duties later
on? Will you be travelling alone or will your
brother be with you?'

Miss Savage gave an angry laugh. 'He's
far too busy, wrapped up in his bridges. . .'

Why did she want to go? thought Louisa
silently. Surely Norway, unless one went
there for winter sports, would be rather an
unsuitable place in which to convalesce? And
she had the impression that the brother wasn't
all that popular with his sister, but that was
no concern of hers.

All the way back to the Royal Southern
she wondered if she had done the right thing,
and knew that when she got back there she
had, for there was a letter from her stepmother, telling her that she was expected
home on her next days off and threatening
to telephone the Principal Nursing Officer if
Louisa didn't go. There were guests coming,
said the letter, and they expected to meet
her, and why hadn't Louisa telephoned for a
week? She was an ungrateful girl. . .

Louisa skimmed through the rest of the
letter; it was merely a repetition of all the
other letters from her stepmother. She would
go home because if she didn't there would be
a lot of unpleasantness, but she wasn't going

to say a word about the new job. Perhaps once she was out of the country and out of reach of her stepmother, she would be left to lead her own life. She wrote a brief reply, scrambled into her uniform and went back on duty.

She told Sister before she went off duty that evening, and later on, after supper, those of her friends who had crowded into her room for a final pot of tea before bed, and her news was received with some astonishment. Louisa had always been considered a rather quiet girl, well liked and ready to join in any fun but unlikely to do anything out of the ordinary. There was a spate of excited talk and any amount of unsolicited advice before they finally went to their own beds.

There were two days to go before her days off. She used them to good advantage, arranging to get a passport and recklessly drawing out quite a big slice of her savings to buy new clothes. Common sense made her pause though before doing that. Supposing Miss Savage changed her mind, she might need the money. . .

But Miss Savage didn't disappoint her; there was a letter confirming the job and a promise to advise her as to travel arrangements in due course. Louisa counted her money and promised herself one or two shopping excursions. But first she had to go home.

She caught an early morning train to Sevenoaks; she could have gone the evening before, but that would have meant another night to be spent at home, but now she would be there well before noon and if there were people coming to lunch, her stepmother wouldn't have much time to talk to her. She got into the Ightham bus and settled down for the four-mile journey, looking with pleasure at the country they were going through. The trees were beginning to turn already and little spirals of blue smoke rose in the cottage gardens where the bonfires had been started. And the village looked lovely too, with its square ringed by old houses. Linda paused to pass the time of day with some of the people who knew her and then walked up the narrow lane leading to her home.

The house was old and timbered and stood sideways on to the lane, surrounded by trees and large gardens. Louisa opened the little gate set in a corner of the hedge, well away from the drive, then walked across the grass and in through a side door leading to a low-ceilinged room furnished with rather old-fashioned chairs and small tables. There were bookshelves on either side of the open hearth and a rather shabby Turkey carpet on the floor. She was half way across it when the door opened and Mrs Evans came in.

'There you are!' Her voice was sharp and held no welcome. 'You should have come last night—Frank was here. And why on earth did you come in this way? You know this room isn't used.' She looked around her with a dissatisfied air. 'So shabby and old-fashioned.'

Louisa put down her overnight bag. 'It was Mother's sitting room,' she said flatly, 'and Father loved it.'

Mrs Evans shrugged thin, elegant shoulders. 'Did you pass your exams?' and when Louisa nodded: 'Thank heaven for that, now perhaps you'll see some sense and settle down. I must say Frank's been patient.'

'I've no intention of marrying Frank, and I'm rather tired of saying so.'

'Then you're a fool. He's got everything—money, that splendid house in the village, that gorgeous car and a villa in Spain. What more could a girl want? Especially when she's not pretty. You're not likely to get another chance like that.' She gave Louisa a quick look. 'You've not fallen in love with one of those young doctors, I hope?'

'No. Why are you so anxious for me to marry Frank Little?'

Her stepmother's answer was a little too careless. 'He's devoted to you and he'll be generous.'

Louisa studied her stepmother; still quite

young, pretty and very elegant; extravagant too. She had been left everything in the will, but Louisa suspected that she had spent most of it during the last three years and had deliberately cultivated Frank Little, hoping for an amenable son-in-law who would pay her bills—and an equally amenable stepdaughter who would marry him.

Well, I won't, thought Louisa. If only her stepmother had been fifteen or ten years younger she could have married him herself. The fact of her father's marriage to a woman so much younger than himself still hurt Louisa. It wouldn't have been so bad if she had loved him. She still wondered at his marrying her; this scheming, clever woman who had twisted him round her little finger and had never forgiven Louisa for not allowing herself to be twisted too. She could think of nothing to say and picked up her bag.

'There are several people coming to lunch,' said Mrs Evans. 'You'd better go and tidy yourself.' She turned and went out of the room ahead of Louisa and crossed the hall to the drawing room, and Louisa went upstairs to her room. While she did her face and tidied her hair she thought about leaving England; she would miss her home, but that was all. She would have to come once more before she went because her stepmother would demand it and if she refused she might wonder why. The temptation to tell her was very great, but Mrs Evans was clever enough to prevent her going. She knew so many people, influential people who could perhaps put a spoke in Louisa's wheel. A car coming up the drive and rather noisy voices greeting each other interrupted her thoughts. She gave her unremarkable person a final inspection in the pier glass, and went downstairs.

The drawing room seemed to have a lot of people in it, but only because they were all talking at once a shade too loudly. Louisa shook hands all round, took the sherry she was offered and made small talk. She knew the five people who had arrived, but only slightly; they were friends of her step-mother's who had never come to the house while her father was alive, but now they were regular visitors. There was one more to come, of course—Frank Little.

He came in presently, a man in his late thirties, rather short and plump, with an air of self-importance which sat ill on his round face with its weak chin. He stood in the door-way for a moment, giving everyone there a chance to greet him, and then went straight to Louisa.

'Your dear mother assured me that you would be here,' he stated without a greeting. 'I know how difficult it is for you to get away.' He took her hand and pressed it. 'I can only hope it's because you knew that I would be here that you came.'

Louisa took her hand away. It was a pity he was so pompous; otherwise she might have felt sorry for him. 'I didn't have to make any special effort to come home,' she told him politely, 'and I didn't know you'd be here.'

Which wasn't quite true; he was always there when she went home. She moved a little way from him. 'What will you drink?'

He sat next to her at lunch, monopolising the conversation in his over-hearty voice, making no secret of the fact that he considered her to be his property.

And he was at dinner too, ill-tempered now because she had escaped that afternoon and gone for a walk—her favourite walk, to Ivy Hatch where the manor house of Ightham Moat stood. She had got back too late for tea and her stepmother had been coldly angry.

And the next day was as bad, worse in fact, for Frank had waylaid her on her way back from the village and rather blusteringly asked her to marry him, and that for the fourth time in a year.

She refused gently because although she didn't like him she didn't want to hurt his feelings. Only when he added angrily: 'Your mother considers me to be the perfect husband for you,' did she turn on her heel and start walking away from him. As she went she said over her shoulder: 'She is not my mother, Frank, and I intend to choose my own husband when I want to and not before.'

He caught up with her. 'I'm coming up to see you this evening—I'm invited for dinner and there'll be no one else there.'

So after tea she went to her room, packed her bag, told her stepmother that she was leaving on the next bus and went out of the house. Mrs Evans had been too surprised to do or say anything. Louisa, leaping into the bus as it was about to leave, waved cheerfully to Frank, about to cross the village square.

She arrived back at the Royal Southern quite unrepentant, prudently asked one of her friends to say that she wasn't in the home if the telephone went and it was her stepmother, and retired to soak in a hot bath until bedtime.

The ward was busy and she spent almost all her free time shopping, so that she was too tired by the end of the day to have second thoughts about her new job. And at the end of the week she received a letter from Miss Savage confirming it, asking her to call once more so that final details might be sorted out and giving her the day and time of their flight.

And this time when Louisa got to the hotel, it was to find her future patient reclining on a chaise-longue and rather more chatty than previously. 'Uniform,' she observed, after a brief greeting. 'You don't need to travel in one, of course, but you'd better have some with you. Dark blue, I think, and a cap, of course. Go to Harrods and charge it to my account.'

'Will you want me to wear them all the time?'

'Heavens, no—you'll get your free time like anyone else. Besides, I shall be going out quite a bit and I shan't want you around.'

Louisa blinked. 'I think I should like to see your doctor before we go.'

Miss Savage shrugged. 'If you must. He's a busy man—you'd better telephone him. I'll give you his number.' She yawned. 'Take a taxi and come here for me—a friend will drive us to Heathrow. Be here by ten o'clock.' She frowned. 'I can't think of anything else. I shall call you by your christian name—what is it? You did tell me, but I've forgotten.'

'Louisa, Miss Savage.'

'Old-fashioned, but so are you. OK, that's settled, then. I'll see you here in ten days' time.'

Louisa got to her feet. She had been going to ask about clothes; after all, Norway would be colder than London, or so she supposed, but somehow Miss Savage didn't seem to be the right person to ask. Louisa said goodbye in her composed manner and went back on duty. After her patients on the ward, with their diagnoses clearly written down and an exact treatment besides, she found Miss Savage baffling. Her doctor would remedy that, however.

But here she was disappointed. Miss Savage's treatment was to be negligible—rest, fresh air, early nights, good food. 'Miss Savage is on Vitamin B, of course, and I shall supply her with nicotinic acid as well. I've already referred her case to a Norwegian colleague who will give you any information you may wish to know. You, of course, realise that she suffers from dyspepsia and a variety of symptoms which will be treated as they arise.'

Louisa listened to the impersonal voice and when it had finished, asked: 'Exercise, sir?'

'Let our patient decide that, Nurse. I'm sure you understand that she'll have days when she's full of energy—just make sure that she doesn't tax her strength.'

'And notes of the case?' persisted Louisa.

'They'll be sent to her doctor in Bergen.'

She put down the receiver. Miss Savage was a private patient, which might account for the rather guarded statements she had just listened to. Certainly, from her somewhat limited experience of similar cases on the wards, the treatment was very much the same, and unlike the patients in hospital, the patient would probably have more say in the matter of exercise and food. As far as Louisa could see, she was going along to keep an eye on Miss Savage, and not much else. But at least it would get her away from Frank.

The thought was so delightful that she embarked on a shopping spree which left her considerably poorer but possessed of several outfits which, while not absolutely in the forefront of fashion, did a great deal for her ego. She went home once more and because it was the last time for a long while, endured her stepmother's ill-humour and Frank's overbearing manner. There was less than a week to go now and she was getting excited. It was a good thing that the ward was busy so that she had little time to think about anything much except her work, and her off duty was spent in careful packing and a great number of parties given as farewell gestures by her friends.

She wrote to her stepmother the evening before she left and posted it just before she got into the taxi, with such of her friends as could be missed from their wards crowding round wishing her luck. Once the hospital was out of sight she sat back, momentarily utterly appalled at what she was doing, but only for a brief minute or so. She was already savouring the heady taste of freedom.

She was punctual to the minute, but Miss Savage wasn't. Louisa, gathering together the bottles and lotions and stowing them tidily in an elegant beauty box, hoped they wouldn't miss the plane. But a telephone call from reception galvanised her patient into sudden energy and within minutes there was a knock on the door and three people came in—a young woman, as elegant as Miss Savage, and two men. They rushed to embrace Miss Savage, talking loudly and laughing a great deal, ignoring Louisa and then sweeping the entire party, complete with bellboys, luggage and an enormous bouquet of flowers, downstairs. Louisa felt that she had lost touch, at least for the moment. Once they were on the plane she would get Miss Savage to rest—a light meal perhaps and a nap. . .

No one spoke to her and they all piled into an enormous Cadillac and roared off towards Heathrow. She sat in the back of the car, with the young woman beside her and one of the men. Miss Savage sat beside the driver, and for someone with a liver complaint who was supposed to take life easy, behaved in a wild and excitable manner, but Louisa realised that it would be useless to remonstrate with her. She was bubbling over with energy, and the man who was driving was encouraging her.

At Heathrow they got out, and to Louisa's horror, they all booked in for the flight. One of the men must have noticed the look on her face, because he patted her on the shoulder. 'Not to worry, Nurse—we're only taking Claudia to Bergen. Once she's there, she's all yours.'

And a good thing too, thought Louisa, watching the gin and tonics Miss Savage was downing once they were in flight. They were travelling first class and the plane was barely half full, which was perhaps a good thing considering the noise she and her friends were making. They had gone quietly enough through Customs. They had arrived with only a few minutes to spare and there had been no time for chat, but once on board they had relaxed. They might have been in their own homes, so little did they notice their surroundings. To Louisa, tired and apprehensive, the flight seemed endless. She heaved a sigh of relief when the plane began its descent and through a gap in the clouds she saw the wooded islands and the sea below, and then a glimpse of distant snow-capped mountains. Just for a moment she forgot her patient and

her problems, and thrilled with excitement.
Here was a new world, and only time would
reveal all its possibilities.

CHAPTER TWO

BERGEN airport was small compared with Heathrow. It took only minutes for them to clear Customs, summon two taxis and start the drive to Bergen. Louisa, sitting in the second car with the elder of the two men, hardly noticed him, there was such a lot to see. The country was wooded and very beautiful and the road wound between trees already glowing with autumn colour. She had been surprised to see on a signpost that Bergen was twelve miles away to the north; somehow she had expected to plunge straight into the town's suburbs. Presently they came to a village and then another, and then after twenty minutes or so, the outskirts of Bergen. Louisa was a little disappointed, for the busy road they were now on seemed very like any other busy road anywhere in England, but only for a moment. Suddenly they were in the centre of the town, skirting a small square park surrounded by busy streets. Her companion waved a vague hand at the window. 'Nice little tea-room there,' he volunteered, 'very handy for the shops—Claudia's got a flat near the theatre.'

Which, while interesting, meant nothing to Louisa.

They turned off a shopping street presently and came upon another small park set in the centre of a square of tall houses, and at its head, the theatre. The taxis stopped half way along one side and they all got out. Miss Savage's flat was on the first floor of a solid house in the middle of a terrace of similar houses, a handsome apartment, well furnished in the modern Scandinavian style, with its own front door in the lobby on the ground floor. A pleasant-looking young woman had opened the door to them and shown them up the short flight of stairs and disappeared down a passage, to reappear presently with a tea tray. Louisa, bidden to pour tea for everyone, did so, and then at Miss Savage's casual: 'Have a cup yourself, Louisa, then perhaps you'd unpack? There's a maid somewhere, see if you can find her,' went to do as she was bid.

The flat was larger than she had supposed. She had opened doors on to three bedrooms, a bathroom and a cupboard before she came to the kitchen. There was another girl here, young and pretty and, thank heaven, speaking English.

'Eva,' she said as they shook hands. 'I come each day from eight o'clock until seven o'clock in the evening. In the afternoon I go for two hours to my home.' She smiled widely. 'You would like coffee?'

Louisa hadn't enjoyed the tea very much. 'I'd love a cup, but I was going to unpack.'

'Then first I show you your rooms and then the coffee. You are the nurse, I think?'

'That's right.' Louisa followed her back down the passage; first her own room, light and airy, well furnished too, with a shower room leading from it, and then her patient's, much larger, with a bathroom attached and a balcony looking out over the square. Louisa, fortified by the coffee and five minutes' chat with Eva, went back there presently and started to unpack. It took quite a time, for Miss Savage had brought a large wardrobe with her; for an invalid she appeared to expect a good deal of social life. Louisa arranged the last scent bottle on the dressing table, arranged the quilted dressing gown invitingly on the bed, and went in search of her patient.

The tea party was still in full swing, only now a tray of drinks had taken the place of the tea and Miss Savage's pale face was flushed. Before Louisa could say anything, one of the men called out: 'All right, nurse, we're just off—got a plane to catch. Look after our Claudia, won't you?' He winked broadly: 'Keep her on the straight and narrow!'

Their goodbyes took another five minutes

and when they had gone the room was quiet again. Quiet until Miss Savage burst into tears, storming up and down the room, muttering to herself, even waving her arms around. All the same, she managed to look as pretty as ever, like a little girl who couldn't get her own way. Louisa's kind heart melted at the sight of her; with a little difficulty she urged her patient to sit down and then sat beside her. 'You're tired,' she said in her quiet, sensible voice. 'It's been a long day, and it's not over yet. Suppose you have a nap for an hour and Eva and I will get a meal ready for you. You haven't eaten much, have you?'

'I want to go home,' mumbled Miss Savage, and buried her head against Louisa's shoulder.

'Then why don't you? We can pack up in no time at all and after you've had a good night's rest we can get a flight back. . .'

'Fool!' declared Miss Savage. 'Do you really suppose I wanted to come? To leave my friends and all the fun. . .'

Louisa, who hadn't taken offence at being called a fool, quite understanding that her companion was suffering strong feelings about something or other, had asked merely: 'Then why did you come, Miss Savage?'

'He made me, of course. I have to live,

don't I, and if he stops my allowance what am I to do?'

'Who's he?' enquired Louisa gently. 'You don't have to tell me, only it might make it easier if you did—perhaps we can think of something.'

'My beastly brother. I detest him—he's mean and high-handed and he made me come here so that he can make sure that I don't spend too much money—and don't have my friends.'

'Very unreasonable,' commented Louisa. 'And what about me? I cost money, don't I?'

'Oh, he pays for you—it was one of the conditions. . .' Miss Savage paused and rearranged her words. 'The doctor said I had to have someone to look after me. . .'

'I should think so indeed!' declared Louisa indignantly. She still didn't like Miss Savage overmuch, but probably her way of life was the result of having a despot of a brother who bullied her. 'Does your brother know you came here today?'

Miss Savage nodded. 'Yes—but you needn't worry, he won't come here. He's miles away—the last I heard of him he was north of Tromso, that's on the way to the North Pole—well, it's a long way beyond the Arctic Circle.'

Louisa produced a handkerchief and wiped Miss Savage's face for her. 'I can't quite see why you had to come to Norway. If your brother wanted you to lead a quieter life, couldn't you have gone to live for a time in the country in England? It would have been much cheaper.'

She couldn't see her patient's face so she didn't see the cunning look upon it. Miss Savage sounded quite convincing when she said: 'But my friends would still come and see me!'

'You'll make friends here,' declared Louisa. 'I thought the town looked delightful, didn't you? In a few days, when you've rested, we'll explore. There are bound to be English people living here.'

Miss Savage sat up. She said: 'You're much nicer than I thought you were. I daresay we'll have quite a good time here. You will help me, won't you? I mean, if I make friends and go out sometimes?'

Louisa answered her cautiously: 'Yes, of course, but you have to rest, you know, but I don't see why we shouldn't work out some sort of a routine so that you can enjoy yourself. No late nights, at least until the doctor says so, and take your pills without fail and eat properly and rest—that's important.'

'It all sounds utterly dreary,' Miss Savage smiled charmingly at her, 'but I'll be good, really I will.'

Suiting the action to the word, she went

to her room, took off her dress and allowed Louisa to tuck her up under the duvet.

Louisa unpacked, consulted with Eva about their evening meal and then, for lack of anything else to do for the moment, went to sit by the sitting room window. There were people in the street below, hurrying home from work, she supposed, taking a short cut across the little park and disappearing round the corner of the theatre at the far end. The sky was clear, but there was a brisk little wind blowing the leaves around and she wondered what it would be like when autumn gave way to winter. From what she had seen of the town she was sure she was going to like it. She hoped she had brought enough warm clothing with her: Miss Savage's luggage had contained thick woollies and a couple of anoraks and fur-lined boots, and there was a mink coat which one of the men had carried for her. . . Her thoughts were interrupted by the telephone and she went to answer it quickly before it disturbed her patient. A man's voice, slow and deep, asking something or other.

'I'm sorry, I don't understand you. . .'

'You are the nurse?'

'I'm Miss Savage's nurse, yes.'

'I should like to speak to her. Her brother.'

'She's resting—we only arrived an hour or so ago. Perhaps you'll ring tomorrow.'

Louisa's voice was cool, but not nearly as cold as the man on the other end of the line.

'I shall ring when it is convenient to me,' he said, and hung up on her, leaving her annoyed and quite sure that he was just about the nastiest type she had ever encountered. Why, even Frank seemed better!

She told Miss Savage later, when that lady, remarkably revived by her nap, joined her in the sitting room.

'And that's the last I'll hear from him—obviously he's no intention of coming to see me.' She sounded delighted. 'If he rings again, Louisa, you're to say that I'm shopping or asleep or something. I'm hungry, have you arranged something or shall I go out?'

'Eva has cooked a meal for us; it's all ready being kept hot. Eva goes in a few minutes.'

'What a bore! Oh, well, you'll have to do the chores.'

It hardly seemed the time to point out that she was a nurse, not a maid; Louisa prudently held her tongue and went to tell Eva that she could dish up.

Miss Savage's vivacity lasted for the whole of the meal, although her appetite, after a few mouthfuls of the excellently cooked cod, disappeared entirely—indeed, presently she got up from the table, leaving Louisa, who was famished, to hurry through her meal, which seemed a shame, for the pudding was good too, and the coffee following it excellent. At least Miss Savage accepted coffee, lying back on the big sofa facing the window, looking suddenly as though she'd been on her feet for days and hadn't slept a wink.

'Bed,' said Louisa firmly, 'a warm bath first—do you take sleeping pills? The doctor didn't mention them. . .'

'There are some in my bag, but I don't think I'll need them tonight.' Miss Savage yawned widely, showing beautiful teeth. 'I'll have breakfast in bed—coffee and toast, and don't disturb me until ten o'clock.'

Later, with her patient in bed and presumably sleeping, Louisa cleared away their supper things, tidied the kitchen ready for Eva in the morning and went back to the window. It was very dark outside, but the streets were well lighted and there were plenty of people about and a good deal of traffic. The pleasant thought struck her that if Miss Savage wasn't to be disturbed until ten o'clock each morning, she would have time to take a quick look round after her own breakfast. She could be up and dressed by eight o'clock and Eva would be in the flat then, so that if Miss Savage wanted anything there would be someone there. She didn't know much about private nursing, but it seemed to her that this case wasn't quite as usual; only the vaguest references had been made to off duty, for instance, and what about her free days? She should have made quite sure of those, but she had been so eager to get the job, and although it might not turn out to be exactly what she had expected at least she was out of England, beyond her stepmother's reach, and moreover, in a country which, at first sight, looked delightful.

She went to bed and slept dreamlessly all night.

She was up and ready for Eva when she arrived, and since Miss Savage hadn't said anything more about uniform, she had put on a pleated skirt and a thin sweater.

Eva was surprised to see her already dressed, but she wasted no time in making coffee and unwrapping the still warm rolls she had brought with her. She shared Louisa's coffee too, sitting at the kitchen table while she told Louisa where the shops were and how to go to them. It wasn't nine o'clock when Louisa, a quilted jacket over the sweater and a woolly cap and gloves, left the flat; there would be time to explore and perhaps she could persuade Miss Savage to go for a short walk once she was up. She crossed the little park as Eva had instructed her and turned into Ole Bull Pass and then

into the main shopping street, Torgalmenning, where the shops were already open,
although there weren't many people about.

Louisa walked briskly down its length,
intent on reaching the harbour Eva said she
simply had to see, promising herself that the
next time she would stop and look in all the
shop windows. It didn't take her long; there
was the harbour, bustling with life, ferries
chugging to and fro, freighters tied up in the
distance. It was overlooked on two sides by
rows of ancient houses, many of them
wooden and all of them beautifully cared for
and most of them converted into shops. She
walked a little way beside the water, looking
across to the mountains in the distance and
then nearer to the neat colourful houses cling-
ing to the skirts of the mountains behind the
town. There was a fish market too, but she
didn't dare to stop to inspect it for more than
a minute or two; quite a different matter from
the fish shops at home, and she had never
seen such a variety. She paused for another
minute to stare across the water at a castle—
she would have to find out about that too. . .
She had no more time; she retraced her steps,
aware that there must be another way back
to the flat, probably shorter—tomorrow she
would discover it.

She had time to change into her uniform
when she got back; there was more chance

of Miss Savage doing as she was asked if she was reminded that Louisa was a nurse.

At exactly ten o'clock, Louisa tapped on the door and went in, put the tea tray down by the bed and drew the curtains. Miss Savage wakened slowly, looking very pretty but just as listless as the previous evening. She sat up slowly without answering Louisa's cheerful good morning, merely: 'What a hideous uniform—it doesn't do anything for you at all, but I suppose you'd better wear it—that doctor's coming this morning.'

'Then you'd better stay in bed when you've had your breakfast,' said Louisa cheerfully, ignoring the bit about the uniform. 'He'll want to examine you, I expect.'

Miss Savage yawned. 'I don't want any breakfast.'

'Coffee? Rolls and butter and black cherry jam?' invited Louisa. 'I'll bring it anyway.'

'Not for ten minutes.'

It was amazing what those ten minutes did for her patient. Miss Savage was leaning back against her pillows, looking quite different, positively sparkling. What was more, she drank her coffee, ate a bit of roll and then went to have her bath without any fuss at all. Louisa made the bed and tidied the room and had Miss Savage back in it seconds before the door bell rang.

Doctor Hopland was elderly, portly and

instantly likeable. His English was almost accentless and he appeared to be in no hurry. He listened to Louisa's rather scant information about her patient, nodded his head in a thoughtful way and observed that beyond keeping an eye on Miss Savage he thought there was little he could do. 'I have had notes of the case,' he told Louisa. 'Unhappily there are many such these days and you will understand that there is not a great deal to be done. Miss Savage is co-operative?'

It was hard to give an answer to that. Louisa said slowly: 'On the whole, yes, but she does like her own way. . .'

'I understand. Well, nurse, all you can do is to persuade her to eat good wholesome food and rest whenever she is tired, and as well as that get her into the fresh air. She is in bed, I take it?'

'I thought you might like to examine her, doctor.'

'Certainly. Shall we do that now?'

Miss Savage submitted very nicely to Doctor Hopland's services, in fact she was so meek that Louisa was astonished, but not nearly as astonished as she was an hour later, when Miss Savage, whom she had left reading a book in bed, came into the sitting room and declared that she was going out to see something of Bergen.

So they spent an hour or two looking at

the shops and Miss Savage bought several expensive trifles and an armful of books which Louisa was given to carry. 'And how about a bottle of sherry in case anyone calls?' asked Miss Savage gaily. 'And don't frown like that, Louisa, I know I mustn't drink it. I wonder where we buy it?'

They couldn't see a drink shop and, on reflection, Louisa couldn't remember having passed one, so she went into the bookshop they had just left and asked one of the assistants.

'The nearest one is on the other side of Torget, quite a walk away, and there are quite a lot of restrictions—you can only buy drinks at certain hours.' She glanced at her watch. 'They're closed now and don't open until this evening.'

Miss Savage's voice was high and peevish. 'I never heard such nonsense—you must get it then, I suppose.'

'Is it so urgent?' asked Louisa. 'I mean, do you know anyone here who's likely to come to see you?'

They were walking back to the flat. 'That's beside the point and no business of yours,' said Miss Savage nastily. The charming mood of the morning had quite gone, as Louisa expected, and she had a difficult afternoon and an even worse evening, with her patient lolling on the sofa, refusing meals and playing the tape recorder far too loudly. It was a relief when she was told to go and buy the sherry.

She didn't hurry. It was good to get away from the flat; besides, she was hungry, for she hadn't been given the time to eat her own meal at midday and when tea came, Miss Savage had demanded this and that so that by the time it had been poured out, it was tepid. So now Louisa whipped into a snack bar, had a coffee and a large satisfying bun, and feeling much better, walked on down to the Harbour, along Torget, with its mediaeval houses lining the pavement, and then turned up the side street whose name she had carefully written down, and found the off-licence.

It seemed a great fuss for one bottle of sherry, she decided as she walked briskly back again. It was cold now, but the shops, although closed, were still lighted and there was still a lot of traffic. She went indoors reluctantly; Eva would be gone by now and if Miss Savage was still so peevish she saw little hope of enjoying a pleasant supper.

Miss Savage was sitting at the window, watching TV and so amiable that Louisa almost dropped the bottle in surprise. What was more, her patient made no difficulties about supper. She sat down to the table and even though she ate almost nothing of it, pushed the beautifully cooked cod round the plate, chatting with the utmost good nature while Louisa thankfully ate. She went to bed presently, leaving Louisa to clear the table and then sit writing letters until she went to bed herself.

On the whole, not a bad day, thought Louisa as she laid her head on the pillow and in no time at all, slept dreamlessly.

And that first day seemed to set the pattern of all their days for the next week. Miss Savage was unpredictable, of course, but Louisa had got used to that by now; she could cope with the near-hysterical condition her patient would work herself into within minutes. She even got her to eat at least a little of each meal and, for a time each day, go for a walk. It was a pity that Miss Savage had no interest in museums and no desire to take the funicular to the top of the mountain behind the town and walk around and admire the view which Eva assured them was spectacular. Louisa promised herself that when she had some free time to herself, she would do just that. There was a restaurant there too, so that she might even possibly have her lunch there. And though the tourist trips had ceased, there were regular small steamers going to Stavanger and Haugesund and several of the fjords not too far distant. Presumably they ran all through the winter. Coming back one evening from posting let-

ters, Louisa decided that with her first pay
packet she would invest in a thicker quilted
jacket; a sheepskin one would have been nice,
but she didn't think she would have enough
money for that. She was certainly going to
buy a couple of thick knitted sweaters with
their matching caps and gloves; she had
already bought wool and needles and
embarked on a long scarf, and judging by the
cold crisp air, she would be glad of it soon
enough.

It surprised her rather that Doctor Hopland
hadn't called to see his patient again. True, he
had told her to telephone if she was worried at
all, and she supposed that there was little
that he could do. She carefully checked her
patient's temperature and pulse each day, saw
that she took her pills and did her best to see
that she led a quiet pleasant life, but she felt
uneasily that she wasn't earning her salary.
On the other hand, if Miss Savage should
take a turn for the worse, at least she would
be there to nip it in the bud and get the doctor
at once.

She found such a possibility absurd when
she got back to the flat. Miss Savage was
sitting in the big chair by the window, playing
Patience with such an air of contentment that
it was hard to imagine she had anything
wrong with her at all. She was charming for
the rest of the evening too and astonished

Louisa by saying that she should have most of the next day to herself. 'Go out about eleven o'clock, once I'm up,' she suggested, 'and don't come back until it begins to get dark— about four o'clock. I shall be fine—I feel so much better, and Eva can get my lunch before she goes, and you know I like to take a nap in the afternoon.'

Louisa looked doubtful. 'Suppose someone calls or telephones during the afternoon—there'll be no one there except you.'

Miss Savage shrugged her shoulders. 'I shan't bother to answer—they can call again, can't they?'

Louisa went to bed quite prepared to find that in the morning her patient would have changed her mind. But she hadn't. Indeed, she got up earlier than usual after her breakfast and urged Louisa to go out as soon as they had had their coffee. 'And mind you don't come back until four o'clock,' she called gaily.

Louisa, walking smartly through the town towards the cable railway, reviewed the various instructions she had given Eva, worried for a few minutes about Miss Savage being by herself and then forgot it all in the sheer joy of being out and free to go where she liked for hours on end.

The funicular first, she had decided, and a

walk once she reached the mountain top, then lunch and an afternoon browsing among the shops. There was a large department store she longed to inspect, but Miss Savage hadn't considered it worth a visit. And she would have tea at Reimers Tea Rooms, which Eva had told her was the fashionable place for afternoon tea or morning coffee. There was a great deal more to see, of course, she would have to leave Bergenhus Castle until the next time, as well as the Aquarium and Grieg's house by the Nordasvann lake, not to mention the museums. She hurried up the short hill which took her to the foot of the funicular, bought her ticket and settled herself in the car with a sigh of pure pleasure.

It was wonderful. She had never experienced anything like it—she had a good head for heights and craned her neck in all directions as the car crawled up the face of the mountain, and at the top she was rewarded by a view of the fjords and mountains to take her breath and when she had got it back again she walked. There were paths everywhere, and everywhere mountains and lakes and scenery to make her eyes widen with delight, and when at last she was tired, she lunched in the restaurant—soup and an omelette and coffee—and then went back down the mountain in the cable car.

It was early afternoon by now, but the flat

wasn't more than ten minutes' walk away from Torgalmenning. Louisa walked slowly, looking in shop windows at the silver jewellery, porcelain and beautifully carved wood, took another longer look at the winter clothes set out so attractively in the boutiques and came finally to Sundt, the department store, where she spent half an hour browsing from counter to counter, working out prices rather laboriously, deciding what she would buy later. It was almost time to go back to the flat; she would have time for a cup of tea first, though. She found the tea room without trouble and sat down at one of the little tables. It was already crowded with smartly dressed women, and Louisa, once she had overcome the few small difficulties in ordering a tray of tea and one of the enormous cream cakes on display, settled down to enjoy herself. She even had an English newspaper, although as she read it England seemed very far away.

She got up to go reluctantly, but content with her day; even the thought that Miss Savage might be in one of her bad moods didn't spoil her feeling of wellbeing. In fact she was quite looking forward to telling her about her outing. This happy state of mind lasted until she opened the door of the flat and started up the stairs. There were voices, loud angry voices, and then Miss Savage's all too familiar sobbing. Louisa took the rest of the stairs two at a time, opened the inner door quietly and made for the half open sitting room door. Miss Savage was lying on the sofa, making a great deal of noise. She had been crying for some time if her puffy pink eyelids were anything to go by and from time to time she let out a small gasping shriek. She saw Louisa at once and cried in a voice thick with tears: 'Louisa—thank God you've come!'

Louisa took stock of the man standing by the sofa. He was tall and spare, with dark hair and an aquiline cast of feature. Moreover, he looked furiously angry, in a towering rage in fact, so that she took a deep breath before she spoke.

'I don't know who you are, but you will be good enough to go at once. Miss Savage has been ill and whoever you are, you haven't any right to upset her in this way.' She held the door open and lifted her chin at him and met dark eyes glittering with rage.

'The nurse?' His voice was crisp. 'I'm Miss Savage's brother, and since this is strictly a family argument, I will ask you to mind your own business.'

'Well, I won't,' said Louisa stoutly. 'You may think you can bully her, but you can't bully me.' She opened the door a little wider. 'Will you go?'

For answer he took the door away from

her and shut it. 'Tell me, what is my sister suffering from, Nurse? Did the doctor tell you? Did she explain when you were engaged? And the doctor here? Has he said anything to you?'

Louisa opened her mouth to speak, but Miss Savage forestalled her by uttering a series of piercing cries and then dissolving into fresh sobs. Louisa brushed past the man, wiped Miss Savage's face for her, sat her up against the cushions and only then turned her attention to him.

'Your sister has a blocked bile duct, she also has dyspepsia. That's a kind of severe indigestion,' she added in case he didn't know, 'I believe you wanted her to come to Norway, presumably to convalesce. We had made some progress during the last week, but I doubt if your visit has helped matters at all. Quite the contrary.'

It was annoying to see him brush her words aside as though they didn't mean a thing. 'You're young. Recently trained, perhaps?'

She supposed she would have to answer him—after all, it was probably he who was paying her fees. 'About six weeks ago.'

His laugh wasn't nice and she flushed angrily. 'Probably you're a good nurse,' he observed in a voice which gave the lie to the statement, 'but you're inexperienced—just what Claudia was looking for.'

'I don't know what you mean.'

'No? I suggest that you put Claudia to bed—she must be exhausted after such a display of emotion. Tell Eva to give her some tea and then come back here. I want to talk to you.'

'I don't think there's much point in that.'

His voice was soft. 'Probably not, but I must point out that I employ you, even if it was my sister who engaged you.' He went to the door and opened it and stood waiting. He had his temper under control by now, and he looked dangerous. Louisa helped Miss Savage on to her feet and walked her out of the room. She said in a voice which shook only very slightly: 'You're despicable, Mr Savage.'

He gave a short laugh. 'Shall we say half an hour, Nurse?'

She didn't answer.

CHAPTER THREE

HALF an hour wasn't nearly long enough in which to regain her cool, thought Louisa, and walked, outwardly composed and inwardly quaking, into the sitting room. Mr Savage was standing at the window, looking out and jingling the loose change in his pockets, and she brightened a little. Perhaps he had recovered from his nasty temper—but when he turned round she saw with regret that she was mistaken; his mood was as black as ever although at the moment he had it under control. She didn't much care for the iciness of his voice when he spoke, though.

'Ah, Nurse, I was beginning to wonder if your courage had deserted you.'

Louisa was, for the most part, a mild-tempered girl, prepared to give rather more than she took, but only up to a point. 'I can't quite see,' she observed in a reasonable voice, 'what I have to be courageous about. True, I dislike being bullied, but a loud voice and a nasty temper don't count for much, when all's said and done.'

She crossed the room and sat down on a small hard chair because it was easier to be dignified like that. Her companion's eyes narrowed. 'Clever, are you?' he wanted to know. 'I've a few questions to ask, and I want truthful answers.'

She stared back at him. 'I can lie with the best of them,' she assured him, 'but never about patients.'

He laughed unpleasantly. 'I'll have to take your word for that. Tell me, why did my sister engage you?'

Her eyes widened. 'Well, she wanted a nurse to accompany her here.'

'There were other applicants?'

'Oh, yes—she told me, but they were all older and she wanted someone younger.'

'Ah, and inexperienced.'

She let that pass. 'Why?'

'I'm asking the questions, Nurse. What's your name?'

'Evans—Louisa Evans.'

'Well, Nurse Evans, presumably you saw my sister's doctor?'

'Naturally, and he gave me my instructions and informed me as to the nature of Miss Savage's illness.'

He gave her a sharp look, eyebrows lifted in faint surprise. 'So you know all there is to know about her?'

She surveyed him coolly. So he thought her incapable of doing her job just because she was young and not greatly experienced, did he? She drew a breath and recited the details of her patient's condition, adding kindly, 'If you don't understand the medical terms I'll explain. . .'

He turned a fulminating look upon her. 'It would be unwise of you to be frivolous, Nurse Evans. I shouldn't try if I were you.'

'I'm not. You're not a doctor, are you?'

'I'm a civil engineer, I build bridges. The reason I asked you that question may not be apparent to you at the moment.'

'It's not.' She got to her feet. 'At least, I daresay you think I'm not old or wise enough to look after your sister. I hope you feel better about it now. She's making a little progress, or was. . . I don't know why you had to upset her, Mr Savage, and I don't want to be impertinent, but your visit hasn't helped much, has it?' Her tongue tripped on, speaking the thoughts she had no intention of uttering. 'I can't for the life of me think why she had to come to Norway. She must have a home somewhere in England; I don't believe she lives in a London hotel; she told me that she came because you made her. . .but there's no reason for that, surely? You work miles away, don't you?'

He had come to stand close to her, his face expressionless, but all the same Louisa had an urge to retreat behind the nearest chair, sternly suppressed. She had the extraordinary feeling that he was on the point of telling her something and at the last minute changed his mind. When he did speak it was to say: 'I wanted her to be nearer to me so that I could visit her easily. I should perhaps explain that we're not the best of friends, Nurse Evans. Claudia is my stepsister, she's only a little younger than I, and we met for the first time when my father married her mother, who had been a widow for some years. We are, in fact, not related—all the same, as we bear the same name I feel some responsibility towards her.' He looked down at her and actually smiled—a thin smile. 'She's been seen by a doctor since you arrived here? I did arrange. . .'

Louisa said impatiently: 'Yes, the doctor came. I have his phone number and he'll call again in a week's time.'

'He gave you no further instructions?' Mr Savage's deep voice sounded curt.

'No, none at all. He told me to carry on as before and to call him if I was worried about anything.'

He moved away from her at last and went to stand at the window again, half turned away from her. 'There seems little point in staying,' he said at length, and turned to look at her, frowning. 'I'm not sure if I'm doing the right thing. . .'

'Well, you are,' said Louisa firmly. 'You

upset Miss Savage and I can't think why you came if you don't get on together—you could have telephoned.'

'My dear good girl, we're talking at cross purposes.' He started for the door. 'I shall telephone from time to time and I shall expect a report from you.' He paused, took a notebook from his pocket, scribbled a number in it and tore out the page. 'You can reach me at this number if you should need to.' He saw her face and gave a crack of laughter. 'Something you don't intend to do; you think I'm a tyrant and a bully. . .'

'As a matter of fact, I do,' said Louisa in a matter-of-fact voice. All the same, the room seemed empty and rather lonely when he had gone.

A small sound made her turn her head; Miss Savage was standing in the doorway. 'He's gone?' She gave a sly smile. 'I'm not really like that, you know, Louisa—making such a fuss—I wanted him to go away, you see.' She twisted her hands together and added in a wheedling voice: 'You're not cross, are you? Was he very rude to you?'

For some reason Louisa found herself saying no when she should really have said yes. She said mildly: 'I think your brother only came to see if you were settled in—I'm sure he has your interest at heart; he wanted to know just how you were. . .'

Miss Savage gave a giggle. 'I bet he did! Did he ask about my friends? The ones who came over with us?'

'No.' Louisa wasn't sure if she liked Miss Savage in this mood.

'Oh, good. I didn't tell him and I didn't have time to ask you not to mention them. He doesn't like them.'

Understandably so, thought Louisa; she didn't like them herself.

'Well, he won't be coming again for ages,' said Miss Savage in a satisfied voice. 'They've just started another bridge somewhere at the back of beyond and once the snow comes travelling around isn't all that easy.'

Louisa thought otherwise. There were domestic flights all over the country; she had collected handfuls of leaflets from a travel agency because she had an inquisitive mind that liked to know about such things. Besides, the friendly woman at the newspaper kiosk had told her that there was a daily steamer that sailed the entire length of the country, right to the Russian border, and back again, calling at dozens of isolated villages. Louisa didn't think that the snow made much difference to the Norwegians—after all, they'd lived there for hundreds of years and by now would know how to deal with their weather. It did put her in mind of something else, though.

'Will we be staying here all winter?'

'Fed up already?' demanded Miss Savage apprehensively. 'I'll make him pay you more. . . Don't go, Louisa.'

Louisa smiled at her patient. 'I don't intend to, and I'm not in the least fed up. I think it's marvellous here. The reason I asked was because I'll have to buy some thicker clothes; it's almost November and I thought I'd get one of those quilted coats and some lined boots.'

'Oh, is that all?' Miss Savage had picked up a copy of *Harpers* and was turning the pages. 'Why don't you get a fur coat? You'll get your wages in just a couple of weeks— Simon said something about it, but I wasn't listening. I expect you know when it's due to be paid? You have to go to the Bergen Bank and ask for Mr. . . He wrote the name down somewhere.' She turned the magazine over: 'Here it is, written on the back— Helgesen.' She added mockingly. 'Simon seemed to think you needed someone to keep an eye on your money, I suppose. The tight-fisted so-and-so!' Her voice became full of self-pity. 'He's got more money than is good for him and he gives me barely enough to live on.'

Probably he was mean, thought Louisa; he certainly was unpleasant enough to add meanness to his faults, but after all, Miss

Savage lived in great comfort and if a mink coat and hand-made Italian shoes were anything to go by, not to mention the luxurious flat in which they lived at present, then her ideas of meanness and Miss Savage's weren't on the same plane.

'My room's in rather a mess.' Miss Savage looked up briefly from her magazine. 'Be a good girl and tidy it for me, will you? I'm exhausted.'

Louisa went. Miss Savage was bone idle, but she had been ill. Louisa knew from experience that getting over an illness was as bad in some ways as actually being in the throes of one. The room looked as though it had endured an earthquake. Miss Savage had wreaked her rage on the soft furnishings to an alarming degree; the bed had its pillows flung in all directions as well as the duvet; there wasn't a cushion in its rightful place and not only had a bottle of perfume been smashed to bits but a jar of one of the expensive creams Miss Savage used had been flung on to the carpet, making a very nasty mess.

Louisa set the room to rights and spent a long time clearing up bits of glass and lumps of face cream. By the time she got back to the sitting room, Miss Savage was asleep, the magazine fallen to the ground. Louisa stood looking at her and thought how very pretty she was, even with her mouth open. She frowned a little, because the prettiness seemed somehow blurred round the edges and was beginning to sag a little, but that was probably because Miss Savage had cried so long and so hard. She would let her sleep for another hour while she went to see what Eva had got for their supper, and presently when she wakened her patient, she was relieved to find that she seemed to have recovered completely from the afternoon's upset. Indeed, Miss Savage spent most of the meal planning their next few days. Rather to Louisa's surprise she suggested that they might visit the Museum of Arts and Crafts— already several of the museums had closed for the winter—and if they enjoyed it, they could visit the rest during the weeks ahead. 'Because there's nothing much else,' she declared. 'Piano recitals, if you like such things, and the cinema—I'll need some new clothes too.' She yawned. 'It's going to be deadly here,' and at Louisa's enquiring look: 'Oh, I can't go back to London, Simon will stop my allowance if I do.' Her voice became plaintive. 'I depend on it utterly.'

'Well, once you're quite well again,' began Louisa, feeling her way, 'could you get a job? You know all about clothes and some of those boutiques must be super to work in.'

She was rewarded with a look of horror

which was quite genuine. 'Me? Work? My dear Louisa, you must be out of your tiny mind! I couldn't possibly—I mean, it's all right for someone like yourself, presumably you expected to have to earn your living; even after you get married your sort usually do a job, don't you? I should die!' And just in case Louisa didn't see her point, she added pettishly: 'I'm still far from well.'

There was no point in arguing. Louisa went away to warm the soup Eva had left and inspect the contents of the casserole in the oven. She still didn't like Miss Savage, but she was sorry for her too; she was missing such a lot of fun. Who would want London anyway? As far as Louisa was concerned anyone could have it, just so long as they left her Bergen to explore. And there was plenty to do: the theatre, cinemas, some wonderful shops and cafés, and, she hoped, the chance to ski; she had asked about that and been told that there were ski slopes not far away where she could be taught. . .once she could get Miss Savage to agree to her having a free day at least once a week. She set supper on the table and made soothing conversation with her patient and presently helped her to bed, since she had become lachrymose again.

But by the morning she was once more her normal self, eating little, it was true, and disinclined to get up, but once she was dressed, Louisa persuaded her to put on her mink coat and its matching cap and go into the town with her. It was a bright day but cold, and they went first to Riemers for their coffee before spending an hour wandering about the shops. The visit to the museum had been forgotten, of course, but Louisa was glad that Miss Savage was at least out of doors, taking an interest in things, and just for once not grumbling; indeed, over lunch she insisted that Louisa should have the afternoon off. 'Because it's getting cold and you'd better get that coat you were talking about. I hope you have enough money, because I've got none,' she finished carelessly.

So after settling her on the sofa with a pile of paperbacks and a light rug, Louisa went off on her own. She knew what she was going to buy. She had seen just what she wanted in Sundt's department store and she went straight there; a quilted jacket with a fleecy lining and a hood. She chose a green one with a brown lining and teamed it up with thick brown slacks and leather boots, then added a thick wool sweater to wear with it and matching mitts and cap. They all added up to a quite formidable sum, but she hadn't spent more than a handful of kroner since they had arrived and pay day wasn't far off. Feeling pleased with herself, she walked the short distance to Riemers and had tea, then started for the flat. It was almost dark by now and the sky had darkened; there had been snow for some weeks in the north of the country, a friendly waitress had told her, and any day now it would snow in Bergen. Louisa sped through the brightly lighted streets, dreaming of skiing and wishing she could get away for long enough to visit some of the nearby islands by the local steamers.

As she neared the flat she saw that its windows blazed with lights and a slight unease jellied into horrible certainty as she opened the door. Miss Savage had visitors; Louisa could hear their loud voices and louder laughter as she went up the stairs. She didn't need to open the door to know who they were.

The three of them turned to look at her as she went in across a room hazy with cigarette smoke. They all held glasses in their hands too, although Miss Savage, sitting on the arm of a chair, had nothing in hers.

Louisa was greeted with shouts of welcome and when they died down Miss Savage called: 'Aren't I good, Louisa? No drinks, but you see how useful that bottle of sherry is being.' She giggled and they all laughed with her except Louisa, who, aware that she was being stuffy, nonetheless was unable to laugh. It was curious that the first thought that entered her head had been concerning

Mr Savage; he would be furious if he knew that these rather wild friends of his step-sister's had arrived; without even asking she knew that he would never approve of them. When the hubbub had died down a little she said hullo in a pleasant cool little voice, refused a glass of sherry and waited to see what would happen next.

It was the woman who spoke—Connie someone or other. She had a strident voice in which she was doing her best to make conciliatory talk. 'How marvellous our Claudia looks, nurse—you're to be congratulated. We just had to see how she was getting on—we're staying a couple of nights at the Norge. You'll let her come out to dinner this evening, won't you? We'll take great care of her.'

It was obvious to Louisa that it wouldn't matter what she said. Miss Savage would go if she had a mind to. She said briskly: 'Of course I don't mind, only don't be too late back, please.' She saw them exchange glances and knew exactly what they were thinking: that she was a bossy young woman who liked ordering people about. If she had said that on a hospital ward they would have accepted it without a murmur. 'And don't wait up,' said Miss Savage. 'Be an angel and run a bath for me, will you? I simply must change.'

Eva brought everyone coffee while they were waiting and presently Louisa excused herself on the plea of consulting with Eva about the next day's meals, and from the kitchen she was called to help Miss Savage fasten her dress, a curiously quiet Miss Savage, hardly speaking and then in a hesitant fashion.

'Do you feel all right?' asked Louisa in a casual voice. 'If you'd rather not go, I'm sure Eva and I can get a meal for you all here.'

Miss Savage was busy pinning a brooch in place. 'Of course I'm all right—don't fuss, for God's sake.' She caught up the mink coat. 'I get little enough fun.'

The flat was gloriously peaceful when they had gone, and presently, when Eva had left for the day, Louisa went along to the kitchen and got her supper, then carried it through to the sitting room and ate it in front of the TV, not really watching it, but it was company. Not that she was lonely; she had plenty to occupy her thoughts, and at the back of her mind a nasty nagging worry that there was something wrong about Miss Savage. Looking back over the days, Louisa realised that her behaviour wasn't consistent; as bright as a button for an hour or so and then listless; bursting into tears for no reason at all and at other times so irritable. She worried round the puzzle like a dog with a bone and came no nearer the answer.

It was almost ten o'clock when the phone rang and she hurried to answer it. Miss Savage in the throes of dyspepsia, or suffering a violent headache. She lifted the receiver and the very last voice she wanted to hear spoke.

'Nurse Evans? I should like to speak to my sister.'

Louisa readjusted her thoughts. 'Good evening, Mr Savage. I'm afraid Miss Savage isn't here—she's out with friends.'

His voice was sharp. 'You know these friends, Nurse?'

She said thankfully: 'Oh, yes—they're from England,' and then wished she hadn't spoken. Miss Savage hadn't wanted him to know about their trip over with her, probably she wouldn't want him to know that they had come again, but it was too late now. The voice, no longer sharp but definitely unpleasant, went on: 'When did they arrive?'

'While I was out this afternoon.' She could have cut through the heavy silence with her scissors.

'You say you know these friends?' It was like being cross-examined.

'I met them in London at Miss Savage's hotel.'

His voice had become silky. 'Ah, yes, just

so. Connie, Willy and Steve—I'm right?'

Louisa gave a great sigh of relief. 'Oh, good, you know them, so that's all right.'

'I know them, Nurse Evans, and it is not all right. These friends are one of the reasons why I wanted Claudia to come to Norway— you must have seen how unsuitable they are for someone in her. . .' he hesitated, 'state of convalescence, and why did you not go with her?' He was coldly condemning.

'Because I wasn't asked,' snapped Louisa. 'I'm not your sister's keeper, you know.'

He said, 'I beg your pardon,' with cool insincerity. 'You don't know how long they're staying in Bergen?'

'They mentioned two nights at the Norge—that's a hotel. . .'

'I'm well aware of that, Nurse. You will endeavour to stay with her as much as poss- ible until they leave. I'm unable to get away from here at the moment, so I must rely on you.' His tone implied that he was expecting the impossible.

She said stiffly: 'I'll do what I can, Mr Savage,' and was rewarded by a disbelieving grunt and the click of the receiver.

Louisa marvelled at his rudeness. 'Almost as bad as Frank in quite a different way,' she observed out loud, and sat down to wait for Miss Savage to come home.

It was almost midnight when she did and

even then her friends seemed to think that they should come in for a last drink, but Louisa, standing at the door, wished them a firm goodnight and shut it equally firmly. Miss Savage had had a splendid evening, she told Louisa, the food had been delicious and she had drunk only one glass of white wine. 'You see how good I am,' she observed as Louisa helped her to bed. 'I'm going to have lunch there tomorrow and drive out to Troldhaugen to see Grieg's house. You won't want to come, of course?'

'I should like to come very much,' said Louisa quickly, aware as she said it that it was the last thing Miss Savage wanted. 'It's kind of you to ask me.'

Out of the corner of her eye she could see Miss Savage's face screwed up with temper.

There was, Louisa decided at the end of the next day, nothing worse than being an unwanted guest. The expressions on the faces of Miss Savage's friends when they called for her in the morning were bad enough, but Miss Savage's ill temper was even worse. Louisa, mindful of Mr Savage's orders, resolutely ignored the cold shoulders, the snide remarks and the sidelong glances—indeed, being a sensible girl, she ate her lunch with pleasure: lobster soup, cod cooked in a delicious sauce with crisp little potatoes and a sea of vegetables, followed by ice cream heaped with honey, fudge and lashings of whipped cream were things to be enjoyed in any circumstances. And afterwards she sat in the back of the hired car, squashed into a window and totally ignored, until they reached Grieg's cottage home on the shore. The house was shut now that it was winter, but it was quite beautiful by the fjord. Miss Savage, her arm in Connie's, wandered off with the two men behind them, calling to Louisa over her shoulder: 'There's a grave somewhere, if you're interested, Louisa, and a stave church in those woods—it's only a few minutes' walk, so I'm told,' she added mockingly. 'Don't worry, we won't go without you.'

So Louisa went off on her own, walking fast because even in the new quilted jacket it was cold. She found the composer's grave, and his wife's beside it, and then followed the path to the church. Its strange pointed roof reminded her of an Eastern temple without the trimmings and she would have liked to see the inside too, but there again the season was over; it would stay quiet and solitary until May when the tourists would come again. She was glad she had seen it in winter, though. If she had the chance, she would come again, preferably when the snow had fallen. And that wouldn't be long now, judging by the thick grey sky, already darkening into an early evening.

Louisa was surprised when Miss Savage refused to spend the evening with her friends. She was, she declared, tired and intended to go to bed early—and indeed, when they had gone she asked, quite nicely too, if Louisa would bring her some tea, and settled on the sofa where she presently fell asleep, leaving Louisa to drink her tea sitting by the window, watching the first of the snow falling. And when she woke up an hour later, she was still pleasant. 'I think I'll go to bed before supper,' she declared, and yawned prettily. 'It's been quite a day—but fun. They're going back tomorrow. Louisa, I want you to go to that wine shop and get another bottle of sherry—I know we don't get many visitors, but there's none in the place now and probably the doctor will have a glass next time he comes.' She got up and stretched her arms above her head. 'I'll have a bath now.' She strolled to the door. 'Was my brother angry when he phoned yesterday?' Her voice was very casual.

Louisa considered. Mr Savage always sounded angry, in her opinion. 'Surprised,' she essayed, 'anxious that you wouldn't get tired or spoil your good progress—no, I don't think he was particularly angry. I'm sorry I mentioned your friends. He asked me where you were, you see, and I had to answer.'

Miss Savage darted a sidelong glance at her. 'Of course,' she smiled. 'You don't have to worry about it—you did tell him they were leaving tomorrow, didn't you?'

'Yes.' Louisa had got to her feet too. 'I'll get your bath going, shall I? Is there anything special you'd like Eva to cook for your supper?'

'I'm not hungry—we had an enormous lunch, lots of coffee and an omelette.'

Butter wouldn't have melted in Miss Savage's mouth for the rest of that evening, and it was the same next morning, which she spent lying in bed reading. It was after an early lunch which she took in her bed that she urged Louisa to go and get the sherry. 'It'll be dark soon,' she pointed out, 'and it's going to snow again—you'd better go while you can.'

So Louisa buttoned herself into her thick jacket, pulled her woolly cap well down over her ears and set out happily enough. It was nice to be out in the clear icy air after the centrally heated flat, and the snow, crisp and white, made the whole town sparkle under leaden skies. There would be more snow and Louisa looked forward to it. The shop was on the other side of the harbour and she walked briskly through the main streets, their shops already lighted, pausing here and there to take a look in the windows. Miss Savage had told her not to hurry back, had even urged her to go and have a cup of coffee on her way back, and there was time enough before tea. Louisa was glad that Miss Savage had elected to stay in bed after the excitement of her friends' visit. They hadn't stayed long enough to do any harm, but on the other hand they hadn't been all that good for her—besides, Mr Savage didn't approve of them. Probably he didn't approve of anything much, only bridges.

The shop was only open for a short time each day. She bought the sherry and started back again, stopping on the way to buy an English newspaper and post some letters. It was still only mid-afternoon and already almost dark, but the streets were alive with people and there was plenty of traffic. She turned down past the Hotel Norge and crossed the little garden in the centre of the square and went into Riemers. It was full and cheerful. Louisa ordered a tray of tea instead of the coffee she usually had, and chose a large cream cake to go with it, eating it slowly while she scanned the headlines of the paper. It was quite dark by the time she went into the streets again and she hurried her steps for the short walk to the flat. Miss Savage's light was on, she saw with relief as she opened the door; probably she was still having her afternoon nap. She went in quietly and peered round the half open door.

Miss Savage was fast asleep, breathing rather thickly, her face flushed. Louisa went close to the bed and bent down to look at her closely and was greeted by a heavy waft of some cloying perfume she didn't like. Disconcertingly, Miss Savage opened her eyes.

'Snooping?' she asked sharply. 'Did my dear stepbrother put you on to that?'

Louisa straightened up. 'Certainly not! He suggested no such thing. You were sleeping so heavily and you looked flushed, I thought you might have a feverish cold.'

Miss Savage replaced the scowl on her face by a sugary smile. 'You really do look after me well, Louisa. I'm just tired and I suppose I've lain in bed too long. I'll get up.'

She was amiability itself for the rest of the evening, praising their meal although she ate almost none of it, and full of more plans for the days ahead, and afterwards as they sat, Louisa with her knitting and she leafing through a magazine, she said something suddenly. 'I forgot something today—you'll have to go to the bank tomorrow morning and get some money for me. You won't need a cheque—they've got instructions to pay the miserable pittance Simon allows me.' She nodded carelessly. 'And isn't it time you had some wages?'

'Next week,' said Louisa, frowning over a difficult bit of pattern.

Presently Miss Savage tossed her magazine down. 'How fast you knit.'

'It's not difficult and very soothing. Would you like to try—or do some of that gorgeous embroidery everyone seems to do here?'

'Lord no—I'd be bored in minutes.' Miss Savage yawned. 'I'm going to bed. You know, the thought of a whole winter here sends me round the bend. I could kill Simon!' She floated away, saying over her shoulder: 'Don't come near me until ten o'clock tomorrow, that's time enough for my coffee.' She didn't say goodnight, but then she wasn't one for the small courtesies of life.

She was bright-eyed and in a splendid mood when Louisa took her coffee in the morning. 'I feel marvellous,' she declared. 'Go and put on your things and go to the bank, will you? I must pay Eva and there are a lot of food bills. . .'

It had been snowing again and it wasn't really light yet, but Louisa found it exciting crunching through the snow in her new boots and despite the winter weather the town looked bright and bustling. The Bergen Bank was an imposing building even from the outside. She climbed the wide steps to its enormous doors and went in, to find it even more so on the inside. It was vast with a lofty ceiling, a great many bright lights, and heavy furnishings. She approached the friendliest-looking clerk at the counter and handed him Miss Savage's note, and was rewarded by an instant smile.

'You need to see Mr Helgesen,' he told her, and pinged a bell beside him, and she was led away down a wide corridor to another lofty room, much smaller this time and furnished with a large desk with a youngish man sitting behind it. He got up as she was ushered in and shook hands, which gave her a chance to study him. A nice face, rugged and good-natured, with blue eyes and close cropped hair. He was stoutly built and a little above middle height, and she took to him at once, and even more so at his friendly voice.

'Miss Evans? Simon Savage told me of you.' He glanced at the note the porter had given him. 'You need money for Miss Savage?'

'Please, she wants to pay her household bills.'

There was a little pause before he said: 'Of course. I'll arrange for you to collect the money she requires. Now sit down for a minute and tell me what you think of Bergen.'

He was the easiest man to talk to. Louisa hadn't realised how much she had missed being able to talk to someone—one couldn't count Miss Savage, who never wanted to talk about anything but clothes and her own discontent. . . She had been talking for several minutes before she stopped herself with an apologetic: 'I'm sorry, I'm wasting your time and Miss Savage will wonder where I've got to.'

They walked to the door together and shook hands, and she felt a small thrill of pleasure when he observed: 'I've enjoyed meeting you, Miss Evans. I hope we shall meet again soon. If you need help of any sort please don't hesitate to call upon me.'

She beamed back at him. 'You're very kind. I'll remember that.'

The money safely in her purse, she went out into the cold again, not noticing it because she was wrapped in a warm glow of pleasure. To stay in Bergen for the entire winter was suddenly inviting.

She was crossing the street in front of Sundt's store, the pavement crowded with shoppers, when she thought she glimpsed the young woman Connie ahead of her, but the traffic lights changed and by the time she was on the opposite side of the pavement there was no sign of her. It couldn't possibly be her, anyway; she and the two men with her had gone back to England several days ago. Louisa, walking happily through the snow back to the flat, didn't think any more about her.

CHAPTER FOUR

LOUISA remembered her mistaken view of Connie later that day. Miss Savage had been remarkably quiet, even drowsy all the afternoon, and over their cups of tea Louisa tried to rouse her interest with undemanding conversation. She was completely taken aback by Miss Savage's reaction to her casual remark that she had imagined that she had seen her friend that morning. Miss Savage's eyes had glittered with rage and she had put her tea cup down so suddenly that most of the tea spilled into the saucer. 'What utter rubbish!' she exclaimed. 'How could you have possibly seen Connie? They're all back home—why can't you mind your own business instead of imagining things which aren't any of your business anyway? just because you don't like my friends. . .'

Louisa, soothing her companion as best she could, found her remarks quite uncalled-for and wondered why she had made them; perhaps she was homesick for London and its life and mentioning Connie had triggered it off. Presently Miss Savage had begun to talk, rather feverishly and about nothing in particular, and Louisa had followed her lead.

The next day or two were passed in a peace and quiet Louisa found surprising and unexpected. Miss Savage was amenable to any conversation made to her and even, when urged, made an effort to eat her meals. The only thing she steadfastly refused to do was to go out. She argued that the snow upset her, that it was far too cold, and that she had no reason to go out anyway. But she insisted that Louisa should go out each day, usually directly after she had taken in her patient's breakfast, 'Because,' as Miss Savage observed, 'it's the one time of day when I don't need anyone—I never get up before eleven o'clock and I like to lie and doze or read.' So Louisa formed the habit of spending the mornings in the town, getting back to the flat round about noon when Miss Savage was usually up and on the point of exchanging her bed for the sofa in the sitting room.

Winter or no, there was a great deal to do, and Louisa happily explored the town in all directions, delighted to find another, not quite as fashionable shopping centre on the farther side of the harbour.

It was a pity that most of the museums were only open in the early afternoons during the winter, but the Bryggens Museum was open for a few hours each day; she went twice to examine the remains of some of the oldest

buildings in Bergen. She went to the Histori-
cal Museum at Sydneshaugen too, which
meant a bus ride to the other side of the town,
but she was beginning to feel so at home now
that she planned several longer excursions if
the weather allowed and Miss Savage would
agree to her having a day off. She had
broached the subject once or twice and met
with evasive answers, and since she had little
to do except act as a companion and see that
her patient took her pills, ate a sufficient
amount and led a quiet life, she felt that she
could hardly complain.

The snow had stopped on the morning she
went to the Bergen Bank to collect her salary.
Rather to her surprise Miss Savage had asked
her to get some more money at the same time.
It had seemed a great deal when Louisa
had handed it over such a short time ago;
apparently housekeeping was an expensive
business in Norway. She went to the same
clerk again and was ushered into Mr
Helgesen's office.

And this time he wasn't alone. Mr Savage
was there, sitting in one of the leather chairs.
Both men got up as she went in, but only Mr
Helgesen crossed the floor to shake hands;
Mr Savage contented himself with a curt nod,
his severe expression not altering one jot.
And two can play at that game, thought
Louisa as she turned a shoulder to him and

addressed Mr Helgesen. 'I think perhaps the clerk made a mistake. I've only come to collect my salary.'

'No mistake, Miss Evans.' Mr Helgesen looked delighted to see her again. 'Mr Savage wished to see you; he has come specially for that purpose.' He added gallantly: 'Of course I wished to see you too.'

She smiled at him rather shyly. 'Thank you. Oh—I'm sorry, I almost forgot, I have another note from Miss Savage. She asked me to get her allowance while I was here.'

The two men exchanged glances. 'Did you not collect it when you were last here?'

'Yes.' Louisa frowned a little. 'She said there wouldn't be any difficulty, that I was just to ask. . .'

'Yes, yes, of course,' said Mr Helgesen soothingly. 'It shall be attended to—if I might have her note?' He went to the door. 'I'll arrange matters with the clerk.'

Louisa didn't much fancy being alone with Mr Savage. 'Couldn't I get it when I get my money?' she enquired, and made for the door too.

'Miss Evans,' said Mr Savage. His voice was quiet but not to be ignored. 'I wish to speak to you.'

She faced him reluctantly and saw his smile. It wasn't a friendly smile; she sat down without a word and waited.

'How is my sister?'

It was a difficult question to answer truthfully, and she hesitated. 'I think she's making slow progress, but she's unpredictable. I mean, her moods vary all the time. But she sleeps well—too much, perhaps—and for the most part she seems content, although she doesn't like living here. She hardly ever goes out, but one can hardly blame her in this weather. . .'

'You go out?'

'But I like it, I think it's lovely, all the snow and the streets lighted. . .'

'Spare me your raptures, Miss Evans. Claudia's friends haven't returned?'

She stared at him in surprise. 'But they went back to England—Miss Savage was very upset.'

'You are sure of that?'

She hesitated. 'Yes—I should have seen them otherwise. I did think I saw Connie— I don't know her name—a few days ago, but the pavement was crowded and I lost sight of her. It must have been a mistake.'

'You didn't enquire at the Norge if she was there?'

Louisa said patiently: 'I've just told you— I don't know her name.'

He stared at her with hard eyes and picked up the phone on the desk—a piece of impertinence, she decided, in someone else's office, too. Who did he think he was?

Of course she didn't understand a word he said, but when he put the receiver down his face was as black as thunder. 'The three of them left yesterday evening.'

She said, 'Oh, dear,' and his lip curled. 'I shall accompany you back to the flat,' he told her. 'Does my sister expect you back immediately?'

'As a matter of fact she told me to have two hours off because she intended to stay in bed until lunchtime.'

'Just so,' said Mr Savage; she wouldn't have been surprised to have seen him grind his teeth and sighed quite audibly with relief as Mr Halgesen came back into the room. He glanced first at Mr Savage and then smiled at her. 'I have told the clerk to let you have Miss Savage's allowance. Mr Savage has opened an account for you here; he thought it wiser, since you were in a foreign country and might not realise. . .it is, I think, rather more expensive here than in England. You can draw any amount you wish, of course,' he laughed a little, 'provided there is still some money there.'

'That's very kind of you, Mr Helgesen.' Louisa turned round to face Mr Savage getting himself into a sheepskin jacket. 'And I expect you meant to be kind too, Mr Savage, but I am capable of managing my own affairs, thank you. I promise you that I shan't run up bills all over the town.'

'And I'm too far away to keep you to that promise. Nurse, shall we go?'

He said something to Mr Helgesen and moved to the door, leaving them together. 'Remember that I will do anything to help you, Miss Evans.' Mr Helgesen engulfed her hand in his. 'Are you ever free in the evening? There is to be a recital of Grieg music at the end of the week, I should very much like to take you.'

'And I'd love to come. But I'd have to ask Miss Savage first—you see, I'd have to leave her alone. . .'

'Perhaps we can think of something. I'll telephone you—if I may?'

'Oh, yes, please.' He really was a dear; what a pity that he and Mr Savage couldn't be in each other's shoes. She shook hands again and walked beside the silent Mr Savage to the desk, where she very defiantly drew out much more money than she needed, and received a bundle of notes for Miss Savage. She quite expected that her companion would make some snide remark, but he remained silent as they went out into the street, and, just as silent, strode beside her on the way back to the flat. Once or twice she was on the verge of some harmless comment, but then she remembered that he had begged her to spare him her raptures. . .

The flat was quiet as she opened the door; usually Eva was bustling round cleaning. Perhaps she was already in the kitchen. . . Louisa went along the passage and pushed open the half open door. Eva wasn't there, but Miss Savage was, sitting at the kitchen table, her bright head on her arms, snoring her head off. On the table was a glass, not quite empty, and beside it a half full vodka bottle. Louisa stood and stared, not quite taking it all in. It wasn't until Mr Savage spoke very quietly over her shoulder that she turned her head to take a look at him.

'You may be a splendid nurse, Miss Evans, highly qualified and skilled and taught everything there is to know about your profession, but one thing no one taught you, and that was to recognise an alcoholic when you saw one.'

'No,' said Louisa, and then: 'Why wasn't I told? The doctors—you. . .'

'I believed that either one or other of the doctors would have briefed you; I had no reason to think otherwise. Indeed, I suggested to Claudia when I arranged for her to come here that she should engage an older woman and that she should be told what exactly was wrong with her patient. Instead, I find a chit of a girl who hasn't a clue. There seemed no point in telling you at first, but when I heard that her three boon companions had been here again, I came down to see you and explain. As you see, I have no need to do so. The matter speaks for itself.'

Louisa gave him a thoughtful look. 'You have no pity, have you?' she observed quietly. 'I think you're the most disagreeable man I've ever met. And now will you carry her through to the bedroom and I'll get her into bed. And then I think you owe me an explanation.'

He didn't answer her, only stooped to lift the still snoring Miss Savage into his arms and carry her down the passage. Louisa, ahead of him, straightened the bedclothes and then tucked her patient up. 'If you'll wait in the sitting room,' she suggested, 'there are one or two things I have to do. If you want coffee there'll be some in the kitchen.'

She didn't wait to see if he would do as she asked but got busy with Miss Savage, bathing her face gently, soothing her, smoothing her hair, wrapping her snugly, and then tidying the room which as usual looked as though it had been ransacked. Presently, when everything was tidy again and she was sure that her patient was still deeply sleeping, she went along to the sitting room. It surprised her that Mr Savage had carried through a tray from the kitchen with the coffee pot and two mugs on it. He poured for them both, gestured her to a chair and asked brusquely:

'Well, what do you want to know?'

Louisa took a sip of coffee. 'All the things that I should have been told in the first place, Mr Savage.'

He sat back in his chair, drinking his coffee with the air of a man who had nothing on his mind. He said carelessly: 'Claudia has been an alcoholic for the last eight years. Everything has been tried—and I mean everything. Once or twice it seemed that she had been cured, but she lapsed. . . These so-called friends of hers—she asks them to get her whisky or vodka or anything else she fancies, and they do. It seems certain that that's why they came to see her again. Surely you would have noticed something?'

'If I'd been warned beforehand, yes. As it was, I believed the doctor's diagnosis.' She added honestly: 'Of course, the diagnosis was correct and I daresay the doctor thought I knew about Miss Savage—it's quite possible, you see, to have all her symptoms for other liver complaints. But now that I know—yes, there were a number of signs I should have been suspicious about.'

'I brought her to Norway because I hoped that away from her friends and the life she led, she stood a better chance of fighting her addiction. It seems I was wrong.'

Louisa put down her cup and met the dark eyes staring at her so coldly. 'Then wouldn't it be a good idea to let her go back to England? She's not happy here; she didn't want to come—she told me that. . .' She paused, seeking a nice way of putting it.

'She had to, otherwise I should have stopped her allowance. Quite correct.' He got to his feet. 'No, I don't intend to let her go back to England. On the contrary, as soon as she is fit enough, she shall travel up to Tromso, and you will accompany her.'

Louisa choked back an instant denial. 'Isn't that a town in the north?'

'Yes. My work is some fifteen miles away from there—a ribbon bridge is being built between two islands. There's a small community there with a few hundred people.' He passed his cup for more coffee. 'You ski?'

'Of course I don't!' She spoke sharply. 'You don't intend that Miss Savage should live there?'

'Indeed I do—she will be under my eye, and so for that matter will you.'

Louisa said with great dignity: 'I believe I can manage my own life without your help.' She added boldly: 'Perhaps your sister would have had a better chance without your interference.'

'You believe in plain speaking, nurse, but I'm afraid your opinion holds no weight with me, so let's keep strictly to the matter in hand.'

'I'll take a look at Miss Savage first,' said Louisa. But that lady was still deep in a snoring slumber.

'You have sufficient warm clothing?' enquired Simon Savage as she sat down again. She told him briefly what she possessed and he said at once: 'You'll need more than that—get a pencil and paper, will you?' And when she had, 'I imagine Claudia has almost nothing suitable; you'll outfit her as well.'

Louisa wrote obediently and then lifted her head to look at him. 'You're not really going to send her all that way? She'll be so lonely, and she doesn't like snow or mountains. . .'

'What a persistent young woman you are! Can you not see that she's almost at her last chance? Perhaps such a drastic step as this will provide that chance. And now be good enough not to argue with me; my mind is made up.'

'Oh, pooh to that,' declared Louisa, and trembled at his icy stare. 'Just supposing she's ill—is there a doctor there?'

'She could be taken to Tromso by motor launch in a very short time. There is a road, of course, but it will be closed until late April— even May.' He smiled thinly at Louisa's look of horror. 'You don't care for the idea?' His voice was silky. 'Perhaps you wish to give up the case, especially as you've been so misled.'

He wanted to be rid of her; any doubts she had been harbouring were instantly squashed. 'Certainly not, Mr Savage! I came to look after your sister, and that's what I intend to do. As you said, such a drastic change in her life might be her salvation, and if there's anything I can do to help her, I shall do it.'

His laugh was quite genuine and she went red with embarrassment and rage. 'I daresay you'll want to be getting back,' she told him stonily, 'and there are several things I want to do before Miss Savage wakes up.'

'Plenty of time for that, she won't stir until this evening or even tomorrow morning.' He walked to the door, picking up his jacket as he went. 'And I'm staying in Bergen until Sunday. I shall be round tomorrow to see Claudia, and by the way, if you want to go out with Helgesen on Saturday evening, I shall be here—my stepsister and I have a good deal to discuss, and I daresay we shall do that better without your well-meaning interference.'

Which remark left her speechless. Eva came back with the shopping presently and Louisa, always a girl to get things settled in her mind, went along to the kitchen, and while lunch was being prepared, got Eva to tell her all she knew about Tromso.

Eva had looked at her in a puzzled fashion. 'But that is a very long way away from here,' she pointed out. 'Why do you wish to know?'

Louisa explained, very carefully, letting it appear that Miss Savage's brother was taking her with him for the benefit of her health.

Eva nodded. 'That is a good idea. It will be beautiful—cold, you understand, but most healthy, and they will have each other, that will be nice.'

'I'm not sure if I was supposed to tell you,' said Louisa doubtfully. 'What happens to your job here?'

'Not to worry, Miss Evans, this flat is rented for six months by Mr Savage and I am to be paid for that time, whether I am needed or not. That was the arrangement.'

'Oh, good.' Louisa got up. 'I'm going to see if Miss Savage is quite comfortable—she doesn't want any lunch, so I'll have mine here with you if I may and you can tell me some more about Tromso.'

Mr Savage returned the following day in the morning. He had been quite right; his stepsister hadn't roused until very late in the evening and then she had been difficult to manage. She had a headache for a start, she felt terrible and she had no wish to do any of the things Louisa suggested. But towards midnight she had quietened down and Louisa had been able to wash her face and hands, change her nightie and re-make her bed. She had gone to sleep almost immediately, which was a good thing, for with one thing and another Louisa was tired out. Disliking some-one, she decided as she put her thankful head on her pillow, was more tiring than anything else she knew of. And it wasn't her patient she was thinking of.

It was Eva who answered the door, took his coat and assured him that she would bring coffee in only a moment. She seemed to like him and Louisa, coming out of Miss Savage's bedroom, couldn't think why. His 'good morning' to her was accompanied by a mock-ing smile and the polite hope that his stepsister was feeling more herself.

'Well, she is,' said Louisa, who had just had a slipper thrown at her by that lady, 'much—but she's also very irritable. Please don't upset her.'

'Oh, I won't. I know what a hangover's like, Nurse. And don't look like that; I also know when to stop.' He sat down by the window. 'The weather's changing. We shall have more snow.'

'Indeed?' queried Louisa coldly. 'You can't see Miss Savage yet, you know.'

'Don't be bossy, Miss Evans. When I've had my coffee I shall see my stepsister—I have a great deal to say to her.'

'She has the most appalling headache. . .'

'Of course she has.' He got up and took the tray from Eva as she came in and smiled so nicely at her that Louisa blinked; she had no idea that he could look like that—quite human. 'Three spoonfuls,' he told her. 'I have a sweet tooth.'

Louisa was glad of her coffee. She had been up early, ministering to Miss Savage, persuading her to drink black coffee, dealing with her headache, ignoring the screams and abuse and ill-temper. Never having been more than slightly tipsy herself, she could only guess how ghastly her patient must be feeling and do her best to get her rational again. She had succeeded to an extent, though. Miss Savage had stopped crying and carrying on and had drunk more coffee and now she was dozing fitfully. 'I won't have her upset,' said Louisa out loud.

'So you have already said,' remarked her companion dryly. 'I suggest that you drink your coffee and go out for a brisk walk, there's nothing like fresh air for clearing the head.' And when Louisa would have protested: 'Have you sufficient money?'

'Plenty, thank you.'

'Very good. We'll discuss clothes and travelling and so on when you return.'

She was dismissed and it would be undignified to protest again. She peeped in at Miss Savage, lying back in her bed with pads on her eyes and the blinds drawn, and then went to her own room and got ready to go out. She was at the door when the telephone rang and when she went to answer it Mr Savage was lying back in his chair, his eyes closed. He looked formidable even like that. Louisa picked up the receiver and found herself smiling because it was Mr Helgesen, wanting to know if she were free on Saturday evening. 'Because if you are, we could have a meal first and then go on to the concert. Could I call for you just after six o'clock?'

'Oh, I'd love that,' said Louisa happily, 'only I quite forgot to ask. . .' She hesitated and glanced at the figure in the chair. 'Miss Savage isn't feeling very well and I hardly like to. . .'

'Women never listen,' observed Simon Savage nastily. 'I remember very clearly telling you that I would be here on Saturday evening. I daresay you're due quite a lot of off duty.'

'Thank you very much,' said Louisa into the phone, ignoring Mr Savage, 'I'll be ready just after six o'clock.' They wished each other goodbye and she rang off. She said rather snappily to the somnolent Simon Savage: 'Of course I listened, but how was I to know you meant it?'

'I always mean what I say—you'll know that in future.'

She flounced out of the room and by a great effort of will, didn't bang the door.

She had a list of shopping to do for Eva and she went first to the fish market, not only to buy fish but to admire the flowers. It amazed her that they were still to be bought in such bitter weather, although at a price she was unable to afford, but just looking at them, spaced out in such an unlikely fashion among the stalls of fish, was a pleasure. She chose her cod with a careful eye, bought a bag of cranberries, went to the little kiosk by the market and bought a *Telegraph*, then started walking away from the harbour towards the shops, stopping on the way to spend ten minutes in one of the many bookshops. There were as many English paperbacks as there were Norwegian—but then she had come to the conclusion that everyone in Norway must speak English as well as their native tongue. She did a little window-shopping after that; obviously she would have to buy quite a few more clothes and it would be as well to price them first. She wondered how long it would be before Miss Savage would feel like shopping, and when they would be going and how. By air, she supposed; there was an excellent domestic service in the country and surely at this time of year it was the easiest way to travel.

It might be the easiest way, but it wasn't

going to be their way. She discovered that
when she got back to the flat, to find Miss
Savage, looking like something just put
through the mangle, sitting back against her
pillows listening to her stepbrother, who was
sitting on the side of the bed, talking to her
in a quiet no-nonsense voice. Without turning
his head, he said: 'There you are—just in
time to hear the arrangements which have
been made. Take off your things and come
in here.'

No please or thank you, grumbled Louisa
to herself, and took her time about tidying
her hair and putting more powder on her nose.
She was rewarded by an impatient frown as
she went into the bedroom and sat down
meekly on the dressing table stool. 'Before
we start, Miss Savage, is there anything
you'd like?' she asked.

Her patient shook her head and then
winced at the pain. 'Who cares what I like?'
she moaned, 'Simon least of all.'

Mr Savage didn't appear to hear this; he
said at once: 'The sooner you come the better,
and since you refuse to fly, I'll arrange
for you to travel on the coastal steamer. It
will probably be rather rough at this time of
year, but the journey only takes five days
to Tromso and you'll see some remarkable
scenery. In—let me see, today is
Wednesday. . .a week's time you'll be met

at Tromso, and as it will be afternoon when you get there, you'd better spend the night there and you can finish the trip by launch.'

'No ice?' asked Louisa a little faintly.

'The Gulf Stream,' said Simon Savage impatiently. 'Inland there's plenty of snow, of course.'

'And are you inland?'

He shook his head. 'An arm of Tromso Sound; a little rural perhaps. We're building a bridge between two islands where it joins the sea, they each have a town and a good scattering of houses but only one road on the larger island.'

It sounded bleak, thought Louisa, and peeped at Miss Savage's face. It looked bleak too. 'It does sound a very interesting journey,' she said bracingly. 'Is there anything to do on board?'

Simon Savage's firm mouth remained unsmiling. 'Nothing at all,' he said blandly.

Miss Savage burst into tears and he got to his feet. 'Perhaps tomorrow we should shop for your clothes,' he observed. 'As you're making this unexpected journey, Miss Evans, and you are employed by me, anything you may need will be charged to my account.'

Miss Savage stopped crying long enough to ask: 'And what about me?'

He turned to look at her from the door. 'When have I ever failed to pay your bills,

Claudia?' he asked and, not waiting for an answer, shut the door.

The doctor came shortly after that, pronounced Miss Savage fit to get up if she felt like it, made out a prescription for the headache and before leaving, followed Louisa into the sitting-room and closed the door.

'Miss Savage should be all right,' he told her. 'We must try again, but with discretion. Allow her a drink with her lunch and dinner, Nurse. One glass of whatever she wishes, that is necessary, otherwise the withdrawal symptoms will be too severe. Later, perhaps, we can cut it down to one glass a day, and eventually to none. It is a pity that she has no incentive—if she were married. . .' He shook his head and sighed, because there was really nothing much that he could do.

'It needs a miracle,' said Louisa again.

She coaxed Miss Savage to eat a little of the light lunch Eva had cooked for her presently and gave her the whisky she asked for, and then to distract her attention from her craving, made a great business of making a list of the clothes they were to buy. Miss Savage even got out of bed towards evening, and though she shivered and shook alarmingly, she spent an hour discussing her wardrobe. No expense was to be spared, Louisa noted, but if Simon Savage was prepared to foot the bills, it was no concern of hers. She tucked her patient up presently, gave her supper and another ration of whisky and then, after her own supper, sat up until midnight until she was quite sure that Miss Savage was soundly asleep.

It was after lunch before Simon Savage came, which was a good thing, because his stepsister had wakened in a bad humour, declaring that she couldn't live unless she had a drink at that very minute and throwing her breakfast tray at Louisa. But somehow, now that she knew what was wrong, Louisa didn't mind too much. True, there was an awful lot of mopping up to be done, but she was beginning to feel sorry for Miss Savage now and even to like her a little. After a good deal of coaxing, Miss Savage consented to get dressed and by the time Mr Savage rang the bell, she was at least approachable.

Mr Savage had taken the precaution of hiring a taxi for the afternoon. It took them from shop to shop and the driver waited patiently outside each one. It certainly made shopping easy, and since Louisa didn't have to worry too much about prices, she began to enjoy herself in a modest way. True, she didn't insist on a fur-lined jacket, a fur cap and suede slacks, but she was quite content with her woollen slacks and the waterproof poplin outfit which, Simon Savage assured her, she would find very useful even if she didn't

ski. He ordered her to buy several woollen
sweaters too and a dark green woollen skirt
with a quilted jacket to go with it. 'And you'd
better have a blouse as well,' he suggested
carelessly. 'Probably we shall go to Tromso
and you'll need them for the hotel.'

Which remark sent his stepsister off into
another small orgy of buying.

On the whole, the afternoon went off
smoothly, and since by the time they got back
to the flat Miss Savage was tired out, Louisa
saw her into bed, took her tea and then tucked
her up for a nap. All this took a little time,
of course, but Simon was still there, in the
sitting room, doing nothing. She felt bound
to offer him tea too, which he accepted with
the air of one who had hoped for something
better but would make do with what he could
get. And when she thanked him stiffly for the
things she had bought, he told her peremp-
torily to say no more about it in such a bored
voice that she drank her tea in silence and
was quite relieved when he went.

Possibly building bridges was conducive
to ill-humour and an inability to tolerate the
shortcomings of those one met outside of this
tricky profession. 'I wonder how they can
make an arch without the middle falling into
the water,' Louisa asked the empty room.
'One day when he's in a good mood, I'll ask
him. Only he never is in a good mood.'

CHAPTER FIVE

MISS SAVAGE was at her most difficult for
the rest of that day, alternately begging for a
drink and abusing Louisa when she didn't get
one, and in between that poking sly fun at
her. 'You never guessed, did you?' she
crowed. 'You thought I was being so con-
siderate, sending you out each morning—
and there we were sitting cosily here—they
brought the drinks with them, of course. You
gave me a fright when you thought you'd
seen Connie—I thought it was all up then,
only you never suspected, did you? I'm
clever, you know. I told the doctor in London
that you knew all about me so there was no
need to say anything to you, and I told the
one here just the same.' She went off into a
peal of laughter. 'I wish I'd seen your face
when you and Simon found me! I had a drop
too much—I didn't mean to fall asleep. But
now you know. . .what are you going to do
about it?' She added pathetically with a complete change of manner: 'You won't leave
me, will you, Louisa?'

'No,' said Louisa, 'I won't, and I don't
know what to do about it anyway—only do

as the doctor tells me. And now if you'd put on that dress that's too long, I'll pin it up and get it sewn.' She went on carelessly: 'Do you think it might be a good idea to go to that nice bookshop we found and get half a dozen paperbacks—just to keep us going until we've discovered our way around Tromso?'

'Tromso's miles away from Simon's work,' said Miss Savage sulkily.

'Not so far, and there's this launch. . . I don't see why we shouldn't go there from time to time, do you?'

'You don't know Simon—he hates anyone to be happy.'

And presently, stitching up the hem of the dress, Louisa began to wonder why Simon Savage should take such a bleak view of life, or was it perhaps that his stepsister made it appear so? But upon reflection, she couldn't recall his smiling, only just that once to Eva. She bit off the thread with small white teeth, but on the whole, she decided, he was better than Frank.

He came the next morning with the tickets for their journey and to tell Louisa that he had arranged for them to be taken by taxi down to the ship. 'She sails at seven o'clock and there'll be dinner on board,' he told her, 'no dressing up or anything like that. If Claudia is feeling off colour I'm afraid you'll have to look after her yourself—there are stewardesses to clean the cabins and so on, but I doubt if their English is very good. How is she?'

'Getting dressed.'

He nodded. 'May I stay for coffee?'

Louisa blinked her long lashes. 'Why, of course—it's your flat, isn't it? I'll ask Eva to hurry up a little.'

He didn't stay long, his visit had been one of duty; he made casual conversation with them both and went with an air of relief. He did pause as he went to remind Louisa that she was going out with Lars Helgesen on the following evening, and would she be good enough to tell Eva that he would be there for dinner with his stepsister.

Lars Helgesen and Simon Savage arrived together, and Louisa, in one of the new dresses, a fine wool jersey in several shades of blue, got up from her chair to greet them. Miss Savage, sulking again because she had to spend a few hours with her stepbrother, was lying on the sofa, wearing a soft woollen rose-coloured housecoat and looking really very pretty despite the deep shadows under her eyes and the downward curve of her mouth.

'Lars Helgesen,' said Mr Savage, 'my sister Claudia.'

Mr Helgesen advanced to the sofa and shook hands, looking bemused, and Louisa,

watching him, had to admit that Miss Savage
did look glamorous even if she was addicted
to the bottle, and certainly was worth a
second look. If only she could cure her. . .
She frowned in thought and changed it to a
smile as Mr Helgesen suggested that they
should go.

Mr Savage hadn't said a word to her, nor
did he as they went out of the room. She had
been going to tell him that Eva had promised
to stay on for a little longer that evening and
serve supper, but if he couldn't be civil
enough to wish her good evening, he could
find out for himself.

'Call me Lars,' said Mr Helgesen. 'I
thought we'd walk, it's not far.' He took her
arm and took her down a side street which
led to the market, where they crossed Torget
into Bryggen and stopped outside one of the
old houses there. 'Here we are,' he declared.
'It is a well known restaurant in the town,
and you shall eat some of their delicious fish.'

It was warm inside, old-fashioned, and the
tables were well filled. Louisa took off her
coat and sat down at the table they were led
to. She felt happy; Lars was a pleasant companion, even on their brief walk she had
discovered that. She looked forward to a
delightful evening in his company.

They had sampled the hors d'oeuvres and
were well into the fish when Lars abandoned

his light chat and asked in a carefully casual voice: 'Miss Savage—Claudia—is she very delicate?' And before Louisa could answer: 'She is so very pretty and so charming, I—I was much struck. . .'

'She's recovering from a complaint which left her rather low,' said Louisa carefully. 'She has her ups and downs though.'

Lars offered her the sauce. 'Yes? She is still so young.'

Just as carefully Louisa agreed.

'Of course Simon has told me something about her—that was necessary so that I might check her account from time to time—it is understandable that so very pretty a lady should wish to spend money.' Louisa murmured something or other and he went on: 'Simon tells me that you are to go to the village where he works. He thinks it will be better for her. I shall miss you—both of you.'

Louisa smiled at his earnest face. 'It does sound a long way off, but I'm sure we shall be all right once we're there,' she assured him. 'Have you been there?'

They talked about a great many things after that, finishing their dinner and walking back to the concert hall, and then sat in companionable silence listening to the pianist playing Grieg's music, and when it was over, walking the short distance back to the flat.

'You'll come in for coffee?' asked Louisa,

and felt a little thrill of pleasure at his eager
'Yes, please!' It was such a pity that they
would have no chance to see each other again,
at least until Simon Savage decided to send
them back to Bergen, and he might not do
that, they might go straight back to England.
It depended on his stepsister, didn't it?

They went up the stairs into the quiet flat
and found Simon Savage standing by the
window looking out into the dark night. His
long lean back had the look of a man
impatient to be gone. Miss Savage was still
lying on the sofa, which surprised Louisa;
she had thought that her patient would have
had more than enough of her stepbrother's
company by now. She turned her head as
they went into the room and smiled, her gaze
resting for a bare moment upon Louisa before
lingering upon Mr Helgesen's face. He
crossed the room to her at once. 'I was afraid
you would be in bed,' he told her, and took
her hand, smiling down at her. Louisa, watching them, allowed the faint, vague idea that
Lars had been getting a little interested in
herself to slide into oblivion. Well, it had
been silly of her to imagine any such thing
in the first place. She looked away and found
Simon Savage's dark eyes bent upon her, and
it was only too obvious from the look on his
face that he had read her thoughts. She
flushed angrily. 'I'll get the coffee,' she

muttered, and escaped to the kitchen.

He followed her. 'A pleasant evening, nurse?' he enquired blandly.

'Yes, thank you.' She went on putting cups and saucers on a tray, not looking at him.

'A nice chap, Helgesen.' He watched her through half closed lids. 'Do you have a boy-friend at home, Louisa?'

If she had been expecting that question she would have been ready with a bright answer; as it was all she could think of to say was 'No.'

'I don't say I'm surprised.' He didn't qualify this remark and she didn't answer it, recognising it as bait to make her lose her temper.

'Will you stay for coffee?' she asked sweetly.

He took the tray from her. 'But of course.'

Before the two men went it had been arranged that Lars should take them in his car to the ship—moreover, Louisa heard him arranging to take Miss Savage out to lunch on the following day. She was sure that Mr Savage had heard it as well, but he didn't say anything, not until he was actually on the point of leaving. He said softly: 'You can safely leave it to me, Nurse.'

It surprised her very much when she returned to the sitting room to hear Miss Savage asking her quite humbly if she would mind her going to lunch with Lars Helgesen. 'And I know what you're thinking, but I promise you I'll not drink anything, only tonic water.' She went on dreamily: 'He's sweet, isn't he?'

Louisa, clearing away the coffee cups, wondered if this was the miracle she had hoped for. If it was, she was going to help it along with all her might. 'He's very nice,' she agreed, 'and now what about bed? You want to look your best in the morning.'

There were only three days before they left, and it seemed to Louisa that Lars Helgesen was either at the flat or taking Claudia Savage out to one meal or another. Louisa had awaited her return from their first date in some trepidation, but she need not have worried. Her patient seemed a changed young woman. True, she still needed a drink twice a day, but her temper was no longer something to be reckoned with and she had stopped throwing things about. Moreover, she had asked Louisa to call her Claudia, which was a great step forward and made for friendlier relations all round.

Of Simon Savage there had been neither sight nor sound. He had returned to his work, she knew, but he had made no attempt to telephone or write, nor had he come to say goodbye. She wondered several times what he had said to Lars about his stepsister;

whatever it was had made no difference to his feelings towards that lady. Louisa packed, did last-minute shopping and laid in a small stock of books against Claudia's boredom during their journey. She foresaw difficult days ahead, for Claudia wasn't going to take lightly to not seeing Lars. It seemed a pity that they couldn't have stayed in Bergen now that there was an incentive for her to give up drinking, and it was even more of a pity that there was no way of getting hold of Mr Savage to tell him so. She could of course telephone him, but she had the feeling that if she did he would listen to her in silence and refuse to change his plans. Perhaps he was bent on punishing his stepsister, perhaps he really did believe that a stay in the north would be the means of curing her. Louisa didn't feel inclined to give him the benefit of the doubt.

Their last day came and with it Lars Helgesen to take them both out to lunch— the Norge Hotel this time, and although he was equally attentive to both of them, Louisa found herself wishing that she wasn't there. The other two had so much to say to each other, although he was careful to keep their talk light and amusing, and Claudia replied in kind, sipping her one glass of white wine as though she had little interest in it. Over coffee Louisa had the bright idea of remembering that she still needed some wool to finish her knitting, and left them together with a promise to meet later at the flat where they would have tea before driving to the dock.

They weren't back when she got in, so she got the tea tray ready and sat down to wait. And when they did arrive, what with saying goodbye to Eva, last-minute packing and messages, there was barely time for them to drink their rather late tea before they had to leave.

On board, Lars went with them down the curved stairs to their cabin, a quite roomy one with a table and chairs as well as two narrow beds. There was a tiny shower room too and a good sized cupboard. Its large window looked out on to the deck alongside and Louisa found it quite perfect, although from the mutinous look on Claudia's face she guessed that her views were not shared. Certainly there was a tremendous difference between the cabin and the comfort of the flat, but there was all they could need. She murmured something about finding out mealtimes, said goodbye to Lars and left them together. She encountered nobody as she made her way back to the main hall. There was the ticket office there and here people were queuing to get their tickets to whichever of the stops they wanted. The ship would call at a number of places, some quite large towns, some fishing villages, some a mere cluster of houses. Louisa could imagine how welcome the sight of it must be, especially during the long winter, bringing supplies and mail and discharging passengers and taking others on.

She edged past a family group, complete with pram, small baby and a large dog, and went up another winding stair. The dining room was quite large with small tables and an air of cosiness, and a door from it led to the stern of the ship where, she discovered, the passengers who were travelling only part of the way could sit. There was a cafeteria there and a small bar where she was delighted to see that no spirits were sold, only wines, sherry and port. There were already a few people sitting about, and she went back the way she had come, out of the door again and into a lounge, running across the fore part of the ship, from side to side, with large windows on all sides. There was no one there either, so she went up another small flight of stairs and found another lounge, exactly like the one below but used, she guessed, for observing the scenery. She stood for a few minutes, watching the ship preparing to sail, craning her neck to see Bergen alongside and behind her, lights shining from the houses perched high on the skirts of the mountains

behind the town. And in front of her the fjord
leading to the open sea. It was a dark evening
and she could see very little; probably it
would be both cold and rough. She went
below presently, studied the meals timetable,
made her way through the increasing number
of passengers back to the cabin and tapped
on the door. Someone had just shouted something over the tannoy which she guessed was
an order for people to go ashore, for she could
feel the engines somewhere under her feet.
They would be sailing at any moment now,
and surely Lars would be gone.

He had, and Claudia was sitting slumped
in one of the chairs, crying. The moment she
caught sight of Louisa she shouted: 'I won't
go, I won't! I want to stay with Lars—it's
cruel of Simon to make me just when I'm
h-happy. . .'

Louisa privately agreed with her. It was
cruel of Mr Savage, but then from what she
had seen of him he possessed very little of
the milk of human kindness. She went and
sat down on the edge of one of the beds close
to Claudia and took one of her hands in hers.
'Look, it's not as bad as you think. Listen to
me—you're much better. You've been trying
hard, haven't you, and each day will be
easier. This place, wherever we're going, is
quiet and very peaceful. You'll sleep well
without pills and start eating properly and

you'll feel so well that you won't be bored or tired of doing nothing. And the quicker you do that, the quicker you'll come back to Bergen. Don't you see, if you improve as much as that, your brother can't refuse to let you return? And Lars will be here, won't he, waiting for you?'

Claudia pulled her hand away pettishly. 'Oh, what do you know about it? You've never been in love, you've no idea what it's like. When you meet someone and you know at once. . .'

'It must be wonderful. I've never been in love, as you say, and perhaps I never shall be, but it's happened to you, hasn't it? And you've got to hang on to it. You're one of the lucky ones.'

Claudia turned round slowly to look at her. 'We haven't much in common,' she said, and laughed a little, 'but for a nurse you're not a bad sort.'

Her face crumpled again. 'Do you really think we'll come back soon? And that Lars likes me as much as he says he does?'

'Yes to both questions.'

Claudia was looking at her face in the little jewelled mirror she carried in her handbag. She said defiantly: 'I told him—I told him I was an alcoholic and he just smiled and said that I didn't need to be any more because he was there. Do you suppose I could be cured, Louisa?'

Louisa paused in her unpacking of an overnight bag. 'Yes, I'm quite sure you can. You see, you've got a good reason now, haven't you, and before you never had that, did you?'

Claudia flung the mirror down on the bed. 'All the same, I shall go mad in this beastly little place we're going to, and if I do it'll be Simon's fault.'

'Do you suppose Lars will come and see you?' asked Louisa, and was rewarded by a return of good humour.

'He promised, but he doesn't know when.' Claudia got up and peered out into the dark outside. 'Have we started?'

'Yes, a few minutes ago. Dinner is at eight o'clock. Would you like a glass of wine before then?'

'Whisky.'

'No, wine. You can't buy spirits on board ship, anyway, it's against the law.'

'Oh, well, wine, I suppose.' Claudia looked round her disdainfully. 'I've never been in such a poky little place in my life before, and I've got to share it with you. I can't bear the idea. . .'

Louisa choked back what she would like to have said. 'It's only for four days—and we shall only sleep here, after all.' She felt the ship dipping its nose into the beginnings of the North Sea, heaving alarmingly. 'And if it's rough you may be glad to have someone here.'

There were barely a dozen passengers in the dining room and the steward led them to a window table where two people were already sitting, and when Louisa said, 'Good evening,' because Claudia was looking annoyed at having to share, she was answered to her relief, in the same language—they were an elderly pair and now that she had time to look at them, American.

They leaned over the table to shake hands. 'Mr and Mrs Foster Kuntz,' they said, beaming, 'and I do believe we're the only English speaking passengers.'

Louisa shook hands and Claudia did the same, ungraciously, and since she had nothing to say, Louisa said: 'Miss Savage is visiting her brother near Tromso. She hasn't been well, and I'm travelling with her.'

'Tromso?' queried Mrs Kuntz. 'That's right in the north. We're going to Trondheim to see our daughter—she's married.'

'To a Norwegian?' asked Louisa hastily, because Claudia was ignoring everyone.

Mrs Kuntz laughed in a jolly way. 'No, he's from the USA, same as us. Got a good job too. We're from Texas—San Antonio, cattle and petroleum; Foster here has done very well from them. We thought we'd have a nice long vacation in Europe and visit Cissie before we go home.'

Louisa said, 'What fun for you both,' and picked up her spoon to start on the soup the steward had set before her. 'Have you enjoyed your trip?'

Mrs Kuntz's answer kept the conversation going in a rather one-sided fashion through the cod steaks and the pudding, so that it wasn't too noticeable that Claudia didn't speak at all. They left the dining room together and Mrs Kuntz whispered: 'Your poor friend—I reckon she must have been good and sick—she hasn't said a word.'

Louisa seized her chance. 'Yes, she has been ill and she's still convalescing. You mustn't mind if she doesn't enter into conversation, she finds it exhausting, and I hope you won't mind if we have our coffee quietly in a corner, because I think she's pretty well exhausted. We'll have an early night; there's nothing much to see anyway, is there?'

Mrs Kuntz laid a kind hand on her arm. 'Sure, my dear, we understand. We'll see you at breakfast.'

Claudia had gone to sit at the opposite end of the saloon, as far away from everyone else as she could manage. As Louisa sat down beside her, she muttered: 'I won't go—it's ghastly, those dreadful people—I'm going to get off at the first stop.' And then: 'I'll kill Simon!'

'Rather pointless,' Louisa said calmly. 'We'd be stuck high and dry miles from any-where and not nearly enough money to get home.'

'I'll telephone Lars.'

Louisa poured their coffee. 'I think Lars loves you very much, and I thought you loved him—I thought you were doing this for him.'

'You mind your own business!' snapped Claudia.

'Well, I do usually,' agreed Louisa matter-of-factly, 'but it seems a shame that you should give in so easily. And Lars wouldn't believe it of you.'

'You know a lot about him, don't you?' Claudia turned a furious suspicious face towards her.

'No, but I think he's a very honest and kind man who wouldn't give his friendship or his affection lightly.'

'My God, you sound pompous!' declared Claudia.

'Yes, I know, but you did ask me, didn't you? And I do want to help you to get. . . well again.'

Claudia gave a small sneering laugh. 'Then you'll be out of a job.'

Louisa said soberly, 'Yes, so I shall.' She hadn't thought about that: somehow the

hospital, her stepmother and Frank had all
faded gently into the past and she couldn't
imagine going back to it.

Despite a disturbed night because Claudia
was unable to sleep, Louisa was up early. It
was still dark when she wakened Claudia and
then put on her thick jacket and went outside
on deck. It was cold, but the sky was clear
and she could see lights ahead—Maloy, a
fishing centre, its harbour crowded with
boats, its modern wooden houses already
dimly seen under the bright lights of the dock.
As they drew nearer she could see too that
their bright red roofs were powdered with
snow, as were the fishing boats. The ship
docked and she watched, oblivious of the
cold, while the mail was slung in its great net
on to the dock, and was loaded with more
mail. They were taking passengers aboard
too, quite a number, bound for farther up the
coast. She would have stayed watching the
busy scene until they sailed, but the breakfast
gong sent her back to the cabin to see how
Claudia was faring.

She was dressed and almost ready, and in
a foul temper. She barely spoke to Louisa,
nodded to the Kuntzes at the table and sat
crumbling toast and drinking coffee while
Louisa had her porridge, egg, cranberry jam
and toast, carrying on a friendly conversation
with their companions at the same time.

'I absolutely refuse to go on deck,' declared Claudia when they were back in their cabin. 'I'm worn out and bored, and what am I supposed to do all day on this ghastly ship?'

Louisa produced a couple of paperbacks, a pack of cards and the latest copy of *Vogue* which she had hidden away in the luggage. 'We'll go to the saloon on the top deck,' she declared, 'and of course you don't have to go out if you don't want to—there'll be plenty to look at through the windows.'

'Mountains and sea. I hope to God there's a comfortable chair. . .'

Claudia refused to face a window; Louisa settled her in a large, well upholstered easy chair in a corner, laid the books on a table beside her and went to take a look from the long window overlooking the bows.

Maloy was already behind them, but she caught sight of a narrow ribbon bridge behind the village. 'Did Mr Savage build any of the bridges along this coast?' she asked.

Claudia shrugged, already deep in *Vogue*. 'Oh, he had something to do with several of them, I believe. I've never been interested.'

The ship was sailing between the coast and protecting skerries, but presently it was the open sea—the Norwegian Sea—and the ship, incredibly sturdy despite its smallness, pitched and rolled its way round the headland of Stad, past the Runde birdrock, just visible to the west, and presently into the calm of Alesund.

'We're stopping here for a couple of hours,' observed Louisa cunningly. 'Shall we go ashore and get some coffee and take a quick look at the shops? Lunch isn't till one o'clock—there's more than an hour. . .'

Claudia was looking pale, although she hadn't complained at the rough trip. She said now: 'Louisa, I must have a drink.'

'OK. You won't be able to get whisky, but there'll be sherry or wine. I'll get our coats.'

The few passengers were already crossing the quayside and making for the town, a stone's throw away. It had been snowing and the wind was icy, but both girls were warmly clad, and once in the narrow busy streets, it was warmer. Louisa found an hotel within minutes and sat Claudia down at a window table in the bar, sipping her coffee while her companion drank her sherry, and then ordering more coffee for them both. Claudia was better after that and Louisa walked her briskly up the main street, looking in its shops, buying an English newspaper and one or two more books before going back to the ship. And there once more she was delighted to see that Claudia looked decidedly better and even made an effort to eat some lunch. What was more, she answered, briefly, it was true, when the Kuntzes spoke to her. The ship sailed while they were drinking their coffee and Louisa watched the little town slide away into the distance. There was a mountain behind the houses; one could drive up to its top by taxi and get a splendid view—something she would have loved to do. . .

It was dark when they reached Kristinasund, and even darker when they docked briefly at Molde, although the sight of the twinkling lights which seemed to cover the mountains behind the town was worth a few cold minutes on deck.

Claudia slept better that night, although it was still rough, and she got up with fairly good grace in plenty of time for breakfast. They were sailing up the fjord to Trondheim where there was going to be a three-hour stop, and this time they were among the first to go ashore. There were taxis on the quayside. Louisa ushered Claudia into one of them, said hopefully: 'The shops, please,' and got in too.

It was a short drive, but Claudia hated walking, although she was happy enough to linger from one shop to the next, while Louisa, longing to visit the Nidaros Cathedral, which Eva had told her on no account to miss, wandered along beside her. Clothes could be bought anywhere in the world, she thought irritably, so why couldn't

Claudia be interested in anything else? They had coffee presently, spent some time in a bookshop and then found another taxi to take them back. A successful morning, decided Louisa, and only two more days to go.

She tucked Claudia up in her bed after lunch and waited until she was asleep before putting on her jacket and going on deck again. The weather was still clear, but there was a grey film on the horizon which she guessed was bad weather of some sort. And it was getting dark again, although there was still a little daylight left as they entered the Stokksund Channel. The Captain had told her at lunch to look out for that—a twisting narrow stretch of water where the ships had to sound their sirens before each turn. Only the thought of a cup of tea sent her back to the cabin to rouse Claudia and go up to the dining room for the simple generous meal.

There were fewer passengers now. The Kuntzes had gone and several others had disembarked at Trondheim and those who had got on in their place were Norwegians. They were in the open sea again and it was rough. Claudia lay down on one of the settees in the saloon and promptly went to sleep, and Louisa got out her knitting. She was enjoying it and she felt reasonably happy about Claudia; with luck she would be able to hand her over to her brother in a much better state of health. Beyond that she didn't intend to worry about anything.

The weather worsened as they worked their way steadily up the coast. By morning there was only the dim outlines of mountains and rugged coast to be seen. It had been too dark on the previous evening to catch a glimpse of the land around, and too dark in the early morning to see the iron globe on top of the rock marking the Arctic Circle, although the ship had sounded her siren as she passed, but the clouds lifted briefly after breakfast, just long enough for her to see the Svartisen Glacier, far away in the distance, remote and terrifyingly high.

They stopped at Bodo during the morning and this time Louisa persuaded Claudia to go with her to see the Cathedral, modern and not very large, but beautiful in its way, and then as a sop to Claudia's impatient company, took her to a hotel where she could have her glass of sherry and then coffee. There were some interesting shops too; Claudia bought herself some silver jewellery—dangling earrings and a thick bracelet, and went back, reasonably good-tempered, to the ship.

There was more open sea in the afternoon and just before the light faded completely Louisa, on deck once more, was rewarded with the sight of the Lofoten Wall on the horizon. It looked a mass of barren rock where no one could possibly live, and yet, two hours later, they had docked by a small quay, and tucked into the formidable mountains towering above them was an equally small village, ablaze with lights, boasting a hotel and several shops. Louisa was enchanted and longed to talk to someone about it. It was incredible to her that people could live out their lives amidst such bleakness and, moreover, make such homelike surroundings for themselves.

She managed to convey something of her feelings to the captain when he came into the dining-room and he nodded his great bearded head.

'We do not mind the loneliness,' he told her, 'and we are happy to live simply. We have electricity, warm homes, plenty of books and all the sport you could wish for.' He twinkled at her. 'It is a long way from London, Miss Evans.'

'Thank heaven for that,' said Louisa decidedly. 'I could live here, I think—it's possible.'

They reached Tromso the next day, stopping at Harstad and Finnsnes during the morning. They could have gone ashore at Harstad, but Claudia was morose and disinclined to do anything, so that Louisa packed for them both, contenting herself with a quick peep at both places as they docked. As they steamed through the narrow waters leading to the city, she noticed that the country had changed. There were mountains crowding in on all sides, but the country had got friendly and there were farms here and there, surrounded by birch trees, and everything powdered with snow. There was nothing to be seen of Tromso yet, there were too many bends in the waterway, but there were houses scattered along the shores of the islands on either side of them. Holiday homes, she guessed, and wondered how one got to them—by boat, presumably, although presently she could see a road close to the fjord's edge running between the houses, although on the other side, although there were houses, some built high into the sides of the mountains, there was no road at all. And presently Tromso came in sight, built on an island in the middle of the fjord. Louisa could see the bridge now, linking it with the mainland, larger and longer than the slender pillar bridge linking Finnsnes and its neighbouring island, but just as impressive. It was a pity that she disliked Simon Savage so heartily, otherwise she could have found out a great deal more about them.

She went below reluctantly. Claudia was sleeping again; she woke her gently, listened calmly to her mounting grumbles, coaxed her into her outdoor clothes and observed:

'You'll be able to telephone Lars this evening.'

It acted like magic. Claudia's scowl turned to self-satisfied smiles and Louisa was able to go and find a steward to deal with their luggage and then go back for Claudia. Mr Savage had said that they would be met at Tromso, but that was all. Louisa debated the choice of staying in one of the saloons until they were found, or going ashore and waiting on the quay—there was bound to be a waiting room there. On the whole, she thought it best for them to go to the saloon and wait. The reception area by the office was full of passengers waiting to disembark. Most of them had boarded the ship at Bodo and Harstad. The quay was thronged with people, presumably waiting for friends or relations or travelling still farther north, and there was a steady hum of voices and a good deal of toing and froing. It was difficult to imagine that they were surrounded by bare mountains and glaciers, snow-bound roads and vast forests. Louisa felt excited and happy, and wished that Claudia could feel the same. She took her arm and pushed her gently into a corner and said: 'Once most of these people have gone, we'll go up to the saloon, it'll be quiet there.'

But there was no need. Someone tapped her on the shoulder and she turned round to find Simon Savage, looking somehow much younger and cheerful. An illusion, of course, for all he did was to nod at her in a casual fashion before asking his stepsister if she was ready to leave the ship. If he uttered one word of welcome, Louisa didn't hear it. She said clearly, 'Our luggage is by the office. We had a very good journey, thank you, but your sister is tired.' She glanced at Claudia, who hadn't uttered a word. 'She should rest as soon as possible.'

Just for a moment he looked at her with narrowed eyes and then surprisingly he laughed. 'Bring Claudia, I'll get the luggage,' he said, and turned away.

Horrible man! thought Louisa, watching him shoulder his way through the crowd. He was wearing a sheepskin coat and knitted cap in bright colours. Probably it was that which made him look different, or perhaps she had hoped he would be. . . She put an arm round Claudia's shoulders.

'Come on,' she said cheerfully, 'let's find some tea.'

CHAPTER SIX

THERE was hard-packed snow on the quayside, and Louisa felt Claudia flinch as they
stepped off the gangway behind Simon
Savage and a short, dark, burly man carrying
two of their suitcases, but they didn't have
far to go. There was a Range Rover parked
close to the ship and they were bidden to get
in while their luggage was piled in beside
them. Louisa barely had time to look around
her and take a last look at the ship before
they had left the quay behind, driving down a
road which curved under a bridge and turned
sharply through warehouses, to turn again
and enter the town over a wide bridge. The
long evening had started, although it was not
yet four o'clock, and the shops were brilliantly lighted in what was obviously one of
the main streets, its broad pavements lined
with bare trees. It ended in an open square
surrounded by shops and along one of its
sides, a large, solid-looking hotel. Mr Savage
parked the car, said over his shoulder: 'This is
where you will spend the night,' and got out.

It was more than she had expected, thought
Louisa as she joined him on the pavement

and waited while he held a hand out to his stepsister, in fact it looked delightful. The thought of a comfortable bedroom, a hot bath and a good dinner brought a sparkle to her eye. Even Simon's growling, 'And you'd better make the most of it,' couldn't spoil her pleasure.

It was just as splendid inside: warm, the foyer close-carpeted and furnished with comfortable chairs and little tables and a pleasant, smiling clerk who welcomed them with friendly warmth. He seemed to know Mr Savage already, for they were whisked away to their rooms with no delay at all; cosy rooms next to each other and with a communicating door and each with its own bathroom. Claudia, who had barely spoken since they had been met, looked around her with a critical eye. 'You wouldn't think they'd be able to manage anything like this in such a godforsaken place,' she observed bitterly. 'You don't suppose people actually stay here, do you? I mean for holidays. . .'

'I believe it's popular in the summer, loads of Norwegians come up here from the south—there's a road all the way, you know.'

'No, I didn't know, and I don't want to.'

'I'll unpack your overnight bag. Mr Savage said something about tea. You'd like some, wouldn't you? Or shall I ask for it to be sent up?'

Claudia had regained some of her old languid manner. 'My dear Louisa, after weeks of nothing but you and my own company, I wouldn't miss a chance to have a look at whatever bright lights there are.'

She turned away to the dressing table and Louisa went back to her own room, where she tidied up her hair, did her face and unpacked her own bag. She got out the green wool skirt and the quilted jacket too and shook out a cream silk blouse to go with them. Presumably they would dine later with or without Simon Savage. She wasn't sure if she wanted him to be there or not.

They went down presently and found him sitting at one of the small tables, the tea tray before him. He got up as they reached him, hoped that they had found their rooms comfortable in a colourless voice and begged someone to pour tea.

'Oh, you do it, Louisa,' said Claudia, 'I'm too exhausted. That fearful voyage! I absolutely refuse to go back by ship.'

Her stepbrother looked up briefly from the *Times* he was reading. 'There are plenty of flights—or the road—when the time comes.'

Claudia drew a hissing breath, but before she could speak, Louisa prudently handed her a cup of tea. She did the same for Simon, then poured her own and sat sipping it until he put his paper down and passed the plate of cakes. He caught her eye as he did so and gave a short laugh.

'You remind me forcibly of my old nanny,' he observed, 'urging me to remember my manners.'

'I haven't said a word, Mr Savage.'

'No, but your eyes did. I can recommend the little round ones with the chocolate icing.'

'And now we're here, perhaps you'll tell us what happens next.' Claudia's voice was sharp.

'We leave tomorrow morning. You can have an hour if you need to do any shopping.'

'I should like to stay here, in this hotel.'

He didn't answer this but observed, 'You're looking better, Claudia, better than you've looked for several weeks. The sea journey did you good—you're half way there, you know. Why not finish it properly this time?'

'I hate you!'

He remained unperturbed. 'Yes, I know, but that's got nothing to do with it.' He glanced at his watch. 'Lars will still be in his office if you want to telephone him.' He waved a hand towards the telephone booth by the reception desk. 'Have you the number?'

She got up without answering and hurried across the foyer, and he handed his cup to Louisa for more tea. 'I must admit you have achieved a good deal in this last week or so,

Nurse. Is Claudia drinking at all?'

'Wine or sherry, mid-morning, and a glass with her dinner in the evening.'

He nodded. 'She's in love with Lars Helgesen, isn't she?'

'Yes.'

Simon passed her the cakes and then helped himself. 'Splendid, we must keep that alive at all costs, it might prove the incentive she has never had.'

Louisa eyed him uncertainly. 'Yes, but supposing he doesn't...would he marry her?'

His look mocked her. 'My dear Louisa, if a man loves a woman—really loves her— he'll marry her. Even a termagant like my dear stepsister.'

He really was beastly; perhaps he was a misogynist.

Claudia came back then, looking considerably happier, but presently she said to no one in particular: 'I don't want to come down to dinner—I'll have something in my room.' She gave her stepbrother a quick look, defying him to argue with her, but all he said was: 'A good idea—I'll get a menu sent up presently.' He looked across at Louisa. 'You will dine with me, Louisa? Shall we say half past seven?'

Claudia had got up and she got up too. 'Thank you, Mr Savage.' She gave him a cool nod and followed Claudia to the stairs.

An hour later she was dressing. Claudia, tucked up in bed, with magazines, books and the most recent papers strewn around her, had chosen her meal and was painting her nails, a long and meticulous business. Louisa, bathed and with her hair newly washed, put on the long skirt, the blouse and the little quilted jacket. They made a nice change after days of wearing slacks and woollies and probably she wouldn't have the chance to wear them again for weeks. She did her face carefully, wishing she was strikingly beautiful, witty and self-assured enough to take the shine out of Mr Savage. If she had had more time she might have given herself an elaborate hairdo, but she doubted very much if he would notice anyway, and what did it matter? They both disliked each other so heartily; she had been surprised that he had suggested dinner together. She went to take a last look at Claudia and found a waiter arranging a prawn cocktail, lamb cutlets and a variety of vegetables, and a delicious-looking pudding on the bedtable. There was a glass of wine there too. Louisa, going downstairs, reminded herself to warn Simon Savage. . .

He was waiting for her in the foyer, very elegant in a dark suit, looking longer and leaner than usual. He also looked ill-tempered, and she sighed. She was hungry for her dinner, but it would be spoilt if he was going to sit in stony silence.

It seemed that he was on his best behaviour, for he offered a drink in a quite friendly voice, and when she ventured to mention the possibility of Claudia ordering something to drink without their knowledge, actually thanked her for saying so. 'Though you have no need to worry,' he assured her carelessly, 'I've taken the necessary precautions.'

And she had to be content with that. She sipped her sherry and looked around her. There were quite a number of people now, all well dressed, which somehow seemed strange when she remembered the miles of barren snowy mountains and the cold, stormy sea they had travelled through. She said: 'I didn't expect this—I mean, all this luxury so far away. . .'

'There's an excellent air service, the coastal express calls every day except Christmas Day, and there's a first class highway running from Oslo to Nord Kapp.'

'No trains?'

He raised amused eyebrows. 'Through or over the mountains, Louisa?' and when he saw her flush, he added more kindly: 'The nearest railway is from Narvik into Sweden, the main line comes as far north as Bodo.'

At least they had found something to talk

about. 'I saw any number of bridges—pillar bridges, as we came.'

'Beautiful, aren't they? Quite a number of islands are no longer isolated, although there are still ferries running in all directions and several local airlines.' He actually smiled at her. 'If you've finished your drink shall we have dinner?'

They had a table by the long window, over-looking the street and the square beyond. There was plenty of traffic still and any number of people. And because the street lights were so bright and numerous, the snow-covered pavements had a charming Christmassy look. Which reminded Louisa to ask: 'Shall we be here for Christmas?'

Simon glanced up from the menu he was studying. 'It depends on several things. Be sure I'll give you plenty of warning. Are you anxious to be in England for Christmas?'

She said: 'Oh, no!' in such a tone of alarm that he asked: 'You like Norway? Have you no family?'

'I like Norway very much,' she told him, and added: 'I'd like soup, please, and then the cod.'

'Trailing a red herring, Louisa, or should I say cod?' and when she didn't answer: 'You have a family?'

He gave their order to the waiter and sat

back waiting for her to answer, his dark face faintly bored.

'A stepmother, no one else. Well, aunts and uncles, but they live a good way away. . .'

'Where?'

'Wiltshire and Cumbria.'

Their soup came and she picked up her spoon, glad of something to do. She didn't think she liked this urbane manner any more than his usual curt behaviour, and she wasn't going to answer any more questions.

'You don't care for your stepmother?'

She looked at him across the elegant little table with its lighted candles. 'No.' She supped the last of her soup. 'I'm not going to answer any more questions.'

He raised quizzical eyebrows. 'My dear girl, I'm making polite conversation.'

'You're cross-examining me. Is your bridge almost finished?'

'Yes, the main work was done before the winter set in; there's not much left to do now, and that mostly under cover.'

'May we see it?' asked Louisa.

'By all means, but I doubt if Claudia will want to do that.' He spoke sourly and gave her such a disagreeable look that she rushed on to the next question.

'Are you going to build any more?'

'Now who's being cross-examined? Yes,

I have a contract for three more bridges, one farther north, the other two in the Lofotens.'

'We stopped there at a very small village—it began with an S. . .'

'Stamsund. You liked it?'

'It was dark, but I would like to have gone ashore. . . Lots of bright lights and—and cosy, if you know what I mean.'

The waiter came with their cod and when he had gone again: 'You surprise me, Louisa, or are you putting on an act for my benefit?'

She paused, fork half way to her mouth. 'An act? Why ever should I bother to do that with you?'

His bellow of laughter sent heads turning in their direction. 'Aren't I worth it?'

'No,' said Louisa roundly, and applied herself to her dinner. She was a little surprised to find that although she disliked him still she wasn't. . .scared wasn't the word— intimidated any more.

The cod was beautifully cooked with a delicious sauce and lots of vegetables. She ate it all up with a healthy appetite and followed it by a soufflé, light as air, while Simon ate biscuits and cheese. They had drunk a white wine with their meal, which was perhaps why she found herself telling her companion about Frank. She hadn't meant to, but somehow his questions had led back to her life in England again—the hospitals where she worked, the villages where she lived and quite naturally from there, Frank. It was only when she glanced at him and caught his dark eyes fixed on her so intently that she pulled herself up short.

'I'd better go and see if Claudia is all right,' she said.

'We'll have coffee first.'

She went back to the lounge with him and drank her coffee and talked about the weather, disliking him very much because she suspected that he was laughing at her. She escaped as soon as she could, thanked him for her dinner and asked what time they were to be ready in the morning.

'Eleven o'clock—and I mean eleven o'clock. Unless Claudia particularly wants to do any shopping, I suggest that she has breakfast in bed. We'll breakfast at half past eight precisely.' He looked down his nose at her. 'You're not one of those silly women who don't eat breakfast, I hope?'

Louisa said pertly: 'Perhaps I should have it in my room, then you won't have the bother of talking to me, Mr Savage.'

'I seldom talk at breakfast, Louisa. It will give me the opportunity of giving you any last-minute instructions should it be necessary.'

She gave him a steely glance, wishing she could think of something dignified and really squashing, but she couldn't—though her 'goodnight' was icy.

Claudia was lying against her pillows, a box of chocolates open beside her, books scattered in all directions. She looked up as Louisa went in and said: 'Oh, hullo—there you are. Has Simon let you off the hook? I've had a lovely evening,' and she stretched her arms. 'Such lovely comfort, and the nicest chambermaid—I got her to fetch me some more books and some sweets. I suppose you're going to tell me to go to sleep now.'

Louisa smiled. 'No, I won't. We're leaving at eleven o'clock in the morning. Would you like breakfast in bed so that you'll have plenty of time to dress? And do you want to go to the shops?'

'No, but you can go for me—I want some more of that hand cream and I'm almost out of nail varnish. I suppose Simon will allow us to come here to shop as often as we want to?'

'I expect so,' said Louisa, thinking it most unlikely. 'I'll be up fairly early, I'll get anything you want and be back in time to do your packing.'

Claudia nodded dismissal. 'OK. See you in the morning.'

Louisa, back in slacks, boots and thick sweater after a night's sleep, and wishful to keep Simon Savage's mood as sweet as possible, presented herself in the dining room exactly on time. Claudia was still asleep and she took the precaution of asking the reception girl to get a menu sent up to her room within the next ten minutes. Claudia couldn't be hurried and Simon had said eleven o'clock and meant it.

He was there now waiting for her, dressed for the cold, she noticed, and she wondered just how remote and bleak their future home was to be. He wished her a perfunctory good morning and waved her to the table along one wall, set out with a vast assortment of food: bread, toast, butter, jam, dishes of fish in various sauces and a great bowl of porridge.

She wandered slowly round and presently joined him at their table, a bowl of porridge in one hand and a plate laden with toast, egg, jam and cheese in the other. He got up and took them from her and asked: 'Tea or coffee?'

'Coffee, please.' And after that she didn't speak, but applied herself to her meal, quite undaunted by the open newspaper Simon Savage held in front of his cross face. It was a pity, she thought, that he always had to look so very disagreeable; life couldn't be all that bad. Perhaps he had been crossed in love? She giggled at the very idea—no woman would dare—and choked on it as the paper was lowered.

'You were saying?' Simon Savage enquired coldly.

'Nothing.' She gave him a sweet smile. 'I don't talk at breakfast either.'

He folded his paper deliberately and very neatly. 'Take care, Louisa, I'm not the mildest of men.'

She poured herself another cup of coffee. 'We don't agree about much, Mr Savage— about that, though, we do! Will I be able to get all I want from that big shop across the square?'

'Sundt? I imagine so, provided it's nothing out of the way.' He glanced at his watch. 'Don't let me keep you.'

Claudia was having breakfast when she went back upstairs. Louisa warned her to get up as soon as she had finished, got into her jacket and woolly cap, and went out of the hotel. The shops were open, although it was still not light, and inside Sundt was warm and brightly lighted. Louisa bought everything on her list and spent ten minutes going from counter to counter. She would have to send her stepmother a Christmas present, she supposed, and cards to her friends at the hospital, as well as the aunts and uncles she so seldom saw. She had written once to her home, and told her stepmother that she was in Norway with a patient, but she had given no address and her friends to whom she had written were sworn to secrecy. She had never felt so free, nor, strangely, so happy.

She would have liked to have lingered in the shop, but a glance at her watch told her that there was little more than an hour before they were to leave. And it was as well that she went back when she did, for Claudia was still lying in bed, doing absolutely nothing. Louisa, by now well versed in the right tactics, persuaded her out of her bed, under the shower and dressed with half an hour to spare, and that would be barely enough time for the elaborate make-up without which Claudia refused to face the outside world. Louisa packed neatly and with speed, rang for their cases to be taken down and left in the foyer, so that Simon Savage's impatience would be tempered, and applied herself to getting Claudia downstairs on time. As it was they were only five minutes late, a fact which Simon silently registered by a speaking glance at the clock.

It was going to be a lovely day, the blue sky turning the snow even whiter than it already was, and as the Land Rover left the city's centre, the mountains came into view once more, their grey bulk almost covered with snow, making a magnificent background to the tree-covered slopes that skirted them. Simon Savage turned off at the bridge at the end of the main street and took a road running alongside the fjord, and presently stopped.

There were fishing boats and motor launches moored here, and Louisa saw the same man who had met the boat with him on the previous day coming to meet them. She half expected Claudia to make a fuss as they got out, but beyond a furious look at the two men she did nothing at all, and they were ushered on board a motor launch without further ado. It was a roomy enough vessel with a fair sized cabin, comfortably warm and well fitted out. Claudia, huddled in her thick clothes, curled up at once on one of the cushioned benches and demanded coffee, and Simon without turning his head told Louisa to pour coffee for them all. 'There's a galley,' he told her curtly. 'You'll find everything there.'

It was a small place, more like a cupboard, but it did hold an astonishing number of things, and the coffee was already bubbling in the percolator on top of the spirit stove. She found mugs, set them on a tray, found milk and sugar too, and went back into the cabin. They were all there; the man introduced as Sven smiled at her as he took his mug, but Simon gave her austere thanks without looking at her, and as for Claudia, she turned her head away.

But when the men had gone, she sat up,

accepted the coffee for a second time and looked around her. 'What a dump!' she declared, looking about.

Louisa, who knew next to nothing about boats, thought it to be the height of comfort, but she knew better than to argue with Claudia; there was a mood coming on, unless she could forestall it. . .

She fetched rugs from a shelf, persuaded Claudia to take off her fur coat and her cap and gloves, and tucked her up cosily. 'You're tired,' she observed. 'Close your eyes and have a nap. I daresay we'll be there by the time you wake up.'

Just for once Claudia forgot to be arrogant. 'It's going to be sheer hell,' she whispered. 'It'll kill me!'

'It'll cure you—think how happy that will make Lars.'

Claudia closed her eyes. 'Do you think it's very silly of me to make plans? Wedding plans, I mean. Do you think he'll risk marrying me? I'm an alcoholic. . .'

'Not any more,' declared Louisa stoutly. 'Now close your eyes and make plans.'

Which Claudia did, and presently slept.

The launch was doing a good turn of speed, although the water was choppy. Louisa peered out of the windows and discovered that she couldn't see much for spray, so she put on her jacket again, pulled her woolly

cap down over her ears and went outside.
Simon Savage was at the wheel, well
wrapped against the cold, but when he saw
her he said something to Sven, who took it
from him and crossed the few feet to the cabin
door. He didn't say anything, only pulled her
hood up and over her cap and tied the strings
under her chin, then kissed her gently.

'You look like a nice rosy apple,' he told
her by way of explanation.

She was too surprised to say anything,
which was perhaps just as well, for he went
on in a matter-of-fact voice: 'If you look
behind you'll see Tromsdaltinden. The snow
came early this year, so it will be a long
winter. Any number of people go there on a
Sunday to ski. There's Finmark to the east,
and in a few minutes you'll be able to get a
glimpse of the Lyngen mountains—these are
islands on the port side, look ahead of you
and you'll see the fjord divides—we take the
left arm, it runs between two islands, and it's
there that we're building a bridge.'

Louisa, oblivious of the icy wind, took the
glasses he handed her and then looked her fill.
'People live along here—I can see houses.'

'Settlements—fishing folk mostly—
they're not far from Tromso, and there are
Hansnes and Karlsoy to the north; small villages, but there's a road to Tromso from
Hansnes. Once the bridge is open it will

shorten the journey to Tromso.' He gave her a long considering look. 'You like it here, don't you?'

'Yes. It must be lovely in the summer.'

'It is. That's when we do most of our work.'

'Do you ever go home between bridges?' The moment she had spoken she was sorry. He turned away from her and said shortly: 'You'd better go inside and see if Claudia is awake; we shall be landing very shortly.'

Louisa went at once. Just for a few minutes she had thought that they were beginning to lose their dislike of each other, and she had to admit that for her part she was on the verge of liking him, ill temper and all, but it was obvious that he didn't share her feelings. Oh, well, once they were ashore, he'd be working, she supposed, and they wouldn't have to see much of him. It struck her then that life might be a little difficult for the next few weeks, with Claudia to keep amused. She would have to think of something to occupy them during the short days. She remembered vaguely that Claudia had told her that she had learned to ski as a child and there would surely be a suitable slope not too far away.

She looked out of the window; there were plenty of mountains, but they all looked quite precipitous. Craning her neck, she could just see the bridge ahead of them; some way off still, graceful and narrow, standing tall on its pillars. She would have liked to have gone back outside and taken a good look, but she suspected that Simon had got fed up with her company and sent her inside unnecessarily soon. A pity, because there was a lot to see now—houses, their painted wood bright against the snow, scattered along the fjord's edge, the mountains at their back doors, and as far as she could see, no road. Racks of cod, minute coves sheltering a fishing boat or two, a solitary church, its short pointed spire covered by snow. . .

She put the coffee pot on the stove to warm up and wakened Claudia. She managed to keep the excitement out of her voice as she said: 'We're almost there,' because she knew that Claudia didn't share that feeling; indeed she groaned and declared that nothing would make her set foot on such a solitary snowbound spot.

'Well, if you don't go ashore here, Lars won't know where to find you,' observed Louisa matter-of-factly, 'and I'm sure it's not nearly as bad as you think. I've some coffee for you, drink it up and get wrapped up again.'

'You're nothing but a bully,' complained Claudia, 'every bit as bad as Simon. I'm hungry.'

'We'll get lunch as soon as we land,'

declared Louisa, and hoped that they would: it wouldn't take much to send Claudia off into one of her moods. They were very close to the land now; through the windows she could see a cluster of houses beyond a small quay, more cod drying on wooden racks and a larger building with 'Hotel' in large letters on its bright yellow painted wall. The houses were brightly painted too, blue and red and pink; they made cheerful spots of colour against the snow and the grey granite mountains all around them.

The cabin door opened and Simon poked his head inside. 'We're here', he told them. 'Come along—Sven will bring the luggage along.'

There was no one on the quay, just a few wooden sheds and a stack of boxes. The road ran left and right and they turned to the left between two rows of small houses. There was a shop and then the hotel, but they went on past it to the last half dozen houses or so. Simon turned off the road here and clumped through the snow to one of these; square, like all the rest, and like its neighbours, standing on its own, facing the fjord, the mountains nudging its small plot of ground. He opened the door and went in shouting something as he did so and turned to hold it wide for them to go in too. The hall was very small with a door on either side, and from one of these an elderly woman came hurrying out.

Simon performed introductions in a perfunctory fashion and added: 'Elsa speaks a fair amount of English; she comes each day and cleans the house and cooks for me.' He opened the other door and ushered them into a small square room, warm from the wood-burning stove against one wall and furnished with simple comfort. 'Get your things off,' he suggested, 'Elsa is bringing coffee, then you can see your rooms before lunch. I'll be out this afternoon, but you'll have enough to do, unpacking and finding your way around.'

The coffee came, hot and delicious, and Sven came in with the bags and sat down to drink his too; and presently Elsa led them upstairs to two small rooms, simply furnished and warm, with bright rugs and curtains. There was a bathroom too, and Louisa, who had expected a lack of modern amenities, was impressed. Claudia wasn't—she went and sat on the edge of her bed, making up her face. 'What a dump!' she declared. 'It's ghastly—we can't all use that poky little bathroom.'

'Don't see why not,' said Louisa cheerfully. 'We don't all want it at the same time, I don't suppose. Let's get tidy and go down to lunch.'

Something Claudia refused to do. 'I'm tired to death,' she moaned, 'I'll have something on a tray and go to bed with a book.'

And nothing Louisa said would change her mind. She left her sitting there and went downstairs and found the table laid and Simon at one end of it, bent over a large map and a bundle of papers. He looked up briefly as she went in. 'Where's Claudia?' And when she explained: 'She can come down for her meals or starve, I don't care which. Tell her that.'

Louisa eyed him with disfavour. 'No, you tell her,' she said quietly, and then: 'You're too hard on her, you know.'

Simon gave her a baleful stare. 'Don't preach to me, Nurse.' But he went past her and up the stairs and presently came down again, looking grim, with a seething Claudia behind him. Louisa made an uneasy third at table, sitting between the two of them, eating her cod and potatoes in a heavy silence.

With a muttered excuse Simon went away the moment he had finished eating, and Claudia burst into tears. Louisa gave her another cup of coffee, allowed her to cry her fill and then suggested that they should go upstairs.

'I'll unpack,' she said with a cheerfulness she didn't feel, 'and you can have a nap or read, and we can have tea here, by the stove.' She urged a reluctant Claudia upstairs, bathed her face for her, settled her under the duvet, found a pile of books and started to put away clothes. By the time she had finished, Claudia was asleep and she was able to go to her own little room and do her own unpacking. That done, she went to look out of the window. It was almost dark, but there were lights in all the houses, making the snow sparkle. Tomorrow she would persuade Claudia to explore a bit—a shop, even a small general stores, would be somewhere to go, and perhaps they could get coffee at the hotel. And she was longing to get a closer look at the bridge. She sighed and pulled the curtains, then went downstairs to look for Elsa and ask about tea.

Claudia had calmed down by tea time and when Louisa, who had been prowling round the little house, mentioned casually that there was a telephone in the hall tucked away in a dark corner under the stairs, she declared that she would ring up Lars at once, but before she could get there, there was a call from him. Louisa, roasting herself by the stove and watching the television programme she couldn't understand, heard Claudia's excited voice and heaved a sigh of relief. The call lasted ten minutes or more, during which time Simon came back, said hullo, in a perfunctory manner, and declared his intention of going across the hall to the small room he used as his office. At the door he paused. 'Any idea how you're going to fill in the time here?' he asked.

'I've brought embroidery and knitting and books for both of us. We'll go out each day—Claudia told me she could ski, but I can't.'

'You can learn—there's an easy slope close by. We'll make up a party on Saturday. The shop has books and the papers come with the postman by launch every third day.'

'And perhaps we could go to Tromso once in a while,' asked Louisa, encouraged by these suggestions.

'Perhaps.' He was non-committal about it. 'Claudia will probably give you the hell of a time.'

'Yes, I expect that, but I expect her to get better too.' She spoke defiantly and he laughed.

'I hope you're right.' His eyes narrowed. 'And understand this; any hint of backsliding and I want to know at once. Is that understood?'

'Oh, I understand you very well,' said Louisa, her voice a little high with suppressed feelings. 'What a very disagreeable man you are, Mr Savage, with your orders and arrogance. I should very much dislike having you as a patient.'

His dark eyes snapped at her. 'You surprise me, Louisa. I should have thought it would have been the very thing, because I would be entirely at your mercy and you could wreak revenge to your heart's content.' His silky voice had a nasty edge to it. He opened the door. 'Perhaps we'd better keep out of each other's way?' he wanted to know.

She agreed stiffly and when she was alone again, wondered why the prospect left her with the feeling that life would be rather dull.

CHAPTER SEVEN

CLAUDIA was still asleep when Louisa went down to breakfast the next morning, to find Simon already at the table, spooning up porridge as though he had a train to catch. He got up as she went in, however, wished her good morning and asked her if she preferred coffee to tea. 'And where's Claudia?' he asked indifferently.

'In bed, asleep. I shall take her breakfast up later.'

She met his cold eyes. 'I see no reason why she should be pampered. I brought her here in the hope that the simple life led here would effect a cure.' He sounded impatient.

'Probably you did,' she said equably, 'but there's no reason to rush things, is there? Why put her back up when there's no need? I shall take her breakfast up.' She began on her porridge and dropped the spoon at his sudden roar.

'Are you defying me, Nurse Evans?'

She sugared her porridge. 'Well, yes, I believe I am,' she told him placidly. 'I don't interfere with your bridges, Mr Savage, I

153

don't think that you should interfere with my nursing.'

'Claudia doesn't need a nurse any more.'

She raised her eyes to his. 'You'd like me to go, Mr Savage? You have only to say so. After all, it's you who pays my wages.'

She watched him getting control of his temper while he helped himself to cranberry jam and took some toast. He said evenly: 'Nurse Evans, you may have *carte blanche* with my stepsister, but I advise you to be very careful. I'm not a man to be crossed lightly.'

'Oh, I can see that,' said Louisa airily, 'but if you'll give me a free hand with Claudia, then I promise I won't interfere with your bridges.'

An unwilling laugh escaped him. 'I've never met anyone quite like you, Louisa.' He started gathering up the papers by his plate. 'And you seemed so quiet, almost timid. . . I shan't be in to lunch.'

She finished her breakfast in deep thought. Obviously he didn't intend to organise any activities for them, that was something she would have to do for herself. She cleared the table and went into the kitchen and under Elsa's kindly eye, prepared a tray for Claudia.

It was still dark outside; she prudently left the curtains drawn, switched on the bedside light and only then wakened Claudia, whose temper, never very sunny in the morning, improved a little at the sight of her breakfast tray.

'However did you manage it?' she asked, and yawned hugely. 'I'm sure Simon said something about eight o'clock. . .'

'Yes, he did, but we agreed that you should have breakfast in bed.'

'Every day?'

Louisa nodded. 'Why not? I've little enough to do, you know. I thought we might go out presently and take a look at that shop and perhaps have coffee at the hotel. . .'

'And then what?' demanded Claudia pettishly.

'I'm going to find out about skiing, I'm dying to learn—do you suppose you could teach me?'

Claudia was buttering toast. 'I suppose I could. God knows where I'll get the energy from—it sounds a fearful bore.'

'Perhaps we could try once or twice, and if I'm quite hopeless I'll give it up.'

Claudia had picked up a magazine and was leafing through the pages. 'OK,' she said without much interest, 'I suppose it'll be something to do.'

Louisa was at the door. 'I suppose Lars Helgesen skis beautifully.' She closed the door gently behind her.

There weren't many people about as they

crunched through the snow towards the shop,
but there was a fair amount of activity on the
quay: a fork lifter stacking large cardboard
boxes, parcels and bundles of all shapes and
sizes being sorted; there were lights everywhere, of course, for it was still not light,
although the sky was clear. Several men went
past them on snow scooters, going out of
sight where the last of the houses clustered
on a bend of the fjord. The bridge lay in that
direction; Louisa dearly wanted to see it, but
she doubted whether Claudia would walk so
far. They turned into the shop and were agree-
ably surprised to find that it housed almost
anything they might need. What was more,
the post had arrived and among the letters
was one from Lars. Claudia tucked it into a
pocket, her pale face pink so that she looked
lovelier than ever, and Louisa vowed that
nothing was going to stop her from making
every effort to cure her of her addiction—
'nothing', of course, was Simon Savage
being tiresome. They spent quite a time in
the shop, delighted to find that there was a
small stock of English paperbacks as well
as a two-day-old copy of *The Times*. They
bought chocolate too and Louisa, finding that
they could speak English, asked the young
woman behind the counter about skiing. Her
questions were met with instant offers of skis,
boots, a guide to show them the way and

someone to instruct her. Louisa explained about Claudia teaching her, but accepted the rest of the offer for the next morning and when she offered to pay met with such a vigorous refusal to take a single krone that she didn't say another word. 'You are family of Mr Savage,' she was told. 'He is our friend and we treat you also as friends—friends do not pay.'

They went to the hotel next and were surprised again. It was a small wooden building, not much bigger than the houses round it, but inside it had a small cosy bar, an even smaller dining room and a much larger room where there was a billiard table, dartboard and a number of small tables and chairs. Louisa guessed that it was used for a great many things during the winter, for there was a small screen hung against one wall and a projector beside it, and in one corner there was a piano.

There was no one else there. They ordered coffee and the proprietor brought it himself and then sat down with them, proving to be a fount of information, imparted in English, which while not fluent, was easily understandable. The post came twice a week, they were told, books and magazines could be ordered at the shop and came at the same time. It was possible to go to Tromso whenever they wished provided the weather wasn't bad. There was a film show every

Saturday evening in that very room and dancing afterwards. And when Louisa observed that there weren't all that number of people to come to it, he laughed cheerfully and told her that the people who lived along the shores of the fjord came in for the evening.

'We are very happy here,' he told her. 'We have the mountains and the fjord and in the summer visitors come and camp along the shore and we are very busy. Besides, there is the bridge. The men who work on it sleep and eat here and go home at the weekends. My hotel is full.'

'Won't it be rather quiet when they go?' asked Louisa.

He looked surprised. 'Oh, no—it will be Christmas.'

They parted, the best of friends, presently, and walked back to the house to find that Elsa had their lunch waiting—soup and bread and a number of little dishes filled with varieties of fish and cheese and pickles. Claudia declared that she was tired, although she had soup and coffee before making herself comfortable on the outsize couch before the stove. Louisa waited for her to ask for a drink, but she didn't, and by the time Louisa had cleared the table she was asleep.

Elsa would be in the house until the evening and was perfectly willing to keep an eye on Claudia. Louisa put on her outdoor

things again and went back through the snow,
past the last of the houses to where the rough
road ended, but there was some sort of path
once she had reached the curve of the fjord
and she followed it carefully in the twilight
which she realised was all there was in place
of the daylight. The water looked cold and
dark, whipped up into waves by a cutting
wind, and she faltered for a moment. Suppose
night descended and she couldn't see the path
to go back by? And then she told herself that
she was silly; the snow scooters had gone
that way; it was well used and surely they
would be returning soon? She pressed on to
the next curve and was rewarded by a sight
of the bridge, brilliantly lighted at each end,
and she could see and hear men working. She
was in two minds whether to go on, but a
few flakes of snow sent her sharply back the
way she had come, very aware of the looming
mountains and the gathering darkness. She
had reached the first house when a snow
scooter skidded to a halt beside her and
Simon Savage got off. He greeted her coldly;
'I shouldn't advise you to go off on your own
until you're sure of the way. Only a fool
would do that at this time of the year. It's
easy enough to get lost.'

'I wanted to see the bridge, and I wasn't
being reckless, Mr Savage. I saw some men

go this way before lunchtime, and I guessed there would be a path.'

He grunted. 'And Claudia?' It was snowing quite fast now; he looked enormously tall and bulky.

'We had a very pleasant morning. There was a letter from Lars Helgesen. We went to the shop and then to the hotel for coffee.' She added defiantly: 'And I asked about skiing.'

'Admirable Louisa! I'm sure you'll deal with skis as competently as you do with everything and everyone else. You have someone to teach you?'

'Claudia.'

He gave a great shout of laughter. 'Of course!'

'And there's no need to laugh like that, it will be something to occupy her. Besides, that nice girl in the shop says her brother will go with us. She arranged it all so quickly. . .'

Simon stood still and looked down at her. 'Of course she did,' he said blandly. 'I'd already told her that you might enquire. Her brother is wholly to be trusted, he may even give you a few tips when Claudia gets bored with teaching you.'

They had reached the house and he parked the scooter in the lean-to and opened the door for her. Louisa took off her things and hung them in the hall, got out of her boots and went upstairs in her stockinged feet, not sure if she was pleased or vexed that he should have bothered to arrange everything for them.

Surprisingly tea was a pleasant little meal, and afterwards Louisa got out a pack of cards and taught Claudia how to play Racing Demon while her stepbrother crossed the hall and shut the door firmly behind him. They met again at supper—lamb chops this time followed by cranberry tart and a great pot of coffee—and Simon was so obviously making an effort to entertain them with light conversation that Louisa took pity on him and helped him out as much as she could. Claudia did no such thing, however, either ignoring him or uttering gibes. Louisa could see him holding back his temper with a restraint which did him credit and prayed earnestly that he might not explode with rage before the meal was over. He didn't: as soon as he could decently do so, he wished them goodnight and went back to his work.

When she went down to breakfast the next morning he wished her good morning with his usual austerity, but added at once: 'You were quite right; breakfast with Claudia at the table would be disaster. It's a pity that we dislike each other so heartily. Perhaps you were right and I shouldn't have brought her here.' He gave her a grim little smile. 'Aren't you going to say I told you so?'

Louisa sat down composedly, helped

herself to porridge and sprinkled sugar with a lavish hand. 'No, I'm not, because I'm sure you were right to do so. It's kill or cure, isn't it?' She frowned. 'I wish I knew more about it—alcoholism, I mean, but she is trying, you know. Is Lars coming to visit her?'

'Yes, but I don't know when. Probably next weekend—he'll fly up to Tromso. I haven't told her.'

She nodded. 'That's three days away. Perhaps we could go skiing today?'

'Why not? It's clear weather. I'll tell them to have everything ready for you at the shop, and arrange for Arne to go with you both.' He got up. 'You'll excuse me?' He was gone.

The morning was a huge success. Claudia, once her skis were strapped on, became quite animated, and she and Arne got Louisa between them bullying and encouraging her in turn, while she tripped up, fell over, crossed her skis and did everything wrong, but at the end of an hour or more she found herself actually in some sort of control of the things and began to enjoy herself. They went back to lunch, glowing with exercise. Claudia very pleased with herself because Arne had complimented her on her grace and speed, and Louisa even more pleased because she had almost got the hang of balancing, and best of all, Claudia had actually enjoyed herself; not once had she complained of boredom or evinced a desire to lie down with a book. She ate her meal with a better appetite and although she declared after it that nothing would make her stir out of doors again that day, she did so in a goodnatured fashion, merely requesting Louisa to make her comfortable on the couch, fetch her a book and a rug, and then go away and leave her in peace.

Fortunately for her own comfort, Louisa had no wish to stay indoors. She wrapped herself up once more and started to walk towards the other end of the road. Not very far, because there were only a handful of houses beyond the one they lived in, but once past these, she found herself walking along the edge of the fjord, going rather gingerly towards the spot where the shore thrust a thin finger into the fjord's water. There was a hut there and she went to peer inside it. Bare now but probably used in the summer, she supposed, and decided to retrace her footsteps to the quay which was after all the heart and soul of the little place. She was standing at its far end, peering down into one of the fishing boats when Simon Savage came to stand beside her. 'You enjoyed your skiing?' he asked, not bothering to greet her.

It surprised her very much that she was glad to see him. 'Very much indeed, and so did Claudia. We thought we'd go again tomorrow.'

'Why not?' He wasn't looking at her, was not indeed the least bit interested. She said rather tartly: 'It's getting cold, I'm going back to the house.'

She hadn't expected him to go with her; they left the quay, went past the shop and when they reached the hotel, a few yards farther on, he stopped. 'Coffee,' he said, and took her arm. 'I know it's teatime, but a cup won't hurt you.'

There were several men in the hotel, sitting at tables, drinking coffee and reading their papers, and Louisa suffered a pang of chagrin as he pulled out a chair at one of these, nodded to her to sit down, said something to the two men already sitting there, and then sat down himself. 'Herre Amundsen, Herre Knudsen,' he introduced them, and then in English: 'Miss Louisa Evans, my stepsister's nurse.'

They were youngish men and probably glad to see a new face, because they talked eagerly about their work at the bridge, their homes in Tromso and their wives and families. They would be moving on soon, they told her, another week or so and the bridge would be opened. And how did she like Norway? they wanted to know. Louisa told them, delighted to find such friendliness.

She drank her coffee, and when Simon ordered her another cup she drank that too, hardly noticing, listening to tales of winter storms, avalanches, the midnight sun, reindeer, the Laplanders. . .all the things she had wanted to know about. If Simon Savage had been more forthcoming she would have asked him days ago; but he had never encouraged her to ask questions, let alone talk. . . He sat back now, content to listen, it seemed, replying only briefly when addressed. Presently he said: 'We'd better go. Wait here while I book a table for Saturday evening.'

'Does it really get so crowded?' asked Louisa, watching him talking to the landlord.

'Very busy—many people come to eat and watch the film and afterwards they dance. A splendid evening.'

Louisa thought that it might not be all that splendid. Lars and Claudia would want to talk to each other, she and her stepbrother would probably not be on speaking terms, and she would be forced to drop inane remarks over the high wall of Simon Savage's indifference—but there would be a film afterwards and she hoped devoutly that the men would outnumber the girls so that she would get a chance to dance. Simon was a write-off as far as dancing was concerned.

She thanked him for the coffee as they

walked the short distance back and he muttered something to her in reply, and beyond
a few necessary words during tea and later at
their supper, he had nothing further to say
to her.

The next few days passed surprisingly
smoothly. They skied every morning, and
now that she had got over her first fright,
Louisa was loving it. Claudia was more or
less docile, even grudgingly admitting that
she wasn't as bored as she had expected to
be; certainly she was looking better and years
younger and since there wasn't a great deal
of daylight, she had less time to spend in
front of the mirror in the mornings and after
lunch she was too healthily tired to do more
than read by the stove. True, there had been
one sticky moment when she had demanded
to go to Tromso that weekend, and since
Simon hadn't told her that Lars was coming,
merely telling her curtly that it wasn't possible, he provoked a burst of temper and tears
which took Louisa an hour or more to calm.
Indeed, she had intervened and told him
severely to go away. He had stared at her for
a long moment before he turned on his heel,
and she had the quite ridiculous feeling that
he was silently laughing.

Lars arrived on Saturday morning while
Louisa was cautiously skiing down a gentle
slope at the foot of the mountains. Claudia

had remained at the top with Arne and it was she who saw Lars first, coming down the slope in fine style to meet him. Louisa, not wishing to be an unwelcome third party, began her patient sideways plodding up the slope again and was halfway there when Simon Savage, coming apparently from nowhere, joined her.

'Keep your skis together and then move your right foot up,' he advised her. She paused to look at him. He did look rather handsome, she had to admit, and not as forbidding as usual. 'Where did you come from?' she wanted to know.

'I fetched Lars from the airport. While he was changing I came across the mountains. . .' He waved a vague arm at the forbidding heights all around them, and she said: 'But there's nowhere to go.'

'Yes, there is, if you know the way. I'll show you one day.'

They had reached the top and Simon said something to Arne, who grinned and sped away back to the shop far below.

'Now,' said Simon, 'let me see what you can do.'

An opportunity to show her prowess; the slope was white and inviting and not quite so frightening any more. Claudia and Lars had disappeared: she would show her companion just how good she was. She launched herself with what she hoped was effortless grace.

Her skis crossed almost at once and she ended up upside down in the snow, quite unable to get up. Simon pulled her to her feet, dusted her down and turned her the right way. 'Now, start again, and forget about impressing me.'

She shot him a very peevish glance and then, surprising herself, burst out laughing. 'Serves me right, doesn't it?' she asked, and launched herself cautiously. And this time she managed very well and even managed to stop at the bottom without falling over again to turn round in time to see Simon Savage sailing down after all with a careless expertise which swamped her with envy.

She had no chance to tell him how good he was. 'Do it again,' he commanded, 'and this time keep your feet together and don't be so stiff—you can bend in the middle, I hope?'

Louisa had a great desire to burst into tears; she had done quite well and he hadn't even bothered to tell her so, only snapped at her about her feet. She muttered crossly: 'Oh, we're not all as perfect as you are.'

'No', he sounded quite matter-of-fact, 'but there's no reason why you shouldn't be in time, provided you work at it. Now, are you going to try again?'

She was cross-eyed with weariness by the time he had finished with her, but she had to

admit that she had learnt to control her feet
and had lost her pokerlike stance. They skied
down the slope for the last time and she stood
quietly while Simon undid her skis for her
and then tossed them over his shoulder with
his own. They found Claudia and Lars at
the house, very pleased with themselves, and
when Claudia said rather pointedly that they
were going to spend the afternoon round the
stove, Louisa declared that she had letters to
write in her room and to her surprise, Simon
observed that since they were going out that
evening he had some work to do after lunch.

Louisa didn't write letters. The room was
warm and comfortable enough but she was
lonely. She got on to the bed presently,
wrapped in the duvet and slept until Elsa
came tapping on the door to tell her that tea
was on the table.

But she was sorry that she had gone down,
for Simon Savage had a cup in his workroom
and the other two, although pleasant enough,
quite obviously didn't want her company.
She was trying to think of some good reason
for taking her cup upstairs with her when the
door opened and Simon came in intent on a
second cup. On his way back to the door he
suggested that she should join him, adding,
presumably for the benefit of the others,
'You're interested in bridges—I've just got

the plans for the next one to be built. Bring your tea with you.'

It seemed the lesser of two evils. She followed him out of the room and when he stood aside went into the room on the other side of the hall. She hadn't been in it before; it was smaller than the sitting room, with a small wood stove, a square table, loaded with rolls of paper, notebooks and, she presumed, the paraphernalia of bridge building, and two or three chairs. He waved her to one of them, and sat down again at the table, where he became totally immersed in a plan he unrolled, she sat sipping her tea, studying the back of his neck; she rather liked the way his dark hair grew. After a couple of minutes' complete silence she suggested: 'Since I'm interested in bridges shouldn't I see the plans?'

Simon lifted his head to look at her and she thought it such a pity that he looked so remote. 'My dear girl, I said that to get you out of the room. I'd not the least intention of showing you anything.'

She felt so hurt that it was like a physical pain inside her. She put down her cup and saucer on the table and got to her feet. 'That was kind of you,' she told him quietly. 'I won't trespass on your—hospitality any longer.'

She had whisked out of the room, giving

him no chance to reply. Not that she had expected him to.

She had a nice cry after that, although she wasn't sure why she was crying, and then had a shower and dressed slowly, ready for the evening. Claudia had told her that she was going to wear a long dress, a lovely woollen affair with a matching stole, so Louisa felt quite justified in putting on the long skirt and the quilted waistcoat. She put on more make-up than usual too and did her hair in a complicated style which she prayed would stay up for the rest of the evening.

Lars, who was staying at the hotel, had already gone there. It only remained for Simon Savage, very stylish in pin-stripes and a silk shirt under his sheepskin jacket, to escort them the very short distance to the hotel.

The dining room was almost full and they went straight to their table, and Louisa, who had been worrying about the drinks, was relieved to find that the men made no effort to go to the bar and drank the tonic and lemon Simon had ordered for them all without a muscle of their faces moving.

The dinner was delicious—thick home-made soup, fish beautifully cooked, and fruit salad, followed by a great pot of coffee. They lingered over it, while Lars, bearing the lion's share of the talk, kept them all laughing, until the film was due to start.

The room was crowded and their entry caused a small stir among the audience, calling friendly greetings, offering them seats. In the end they settled in the middle of a row of chairs half way back from the screen, Claudia and Louisa in the middle, the men on either side of them. The film was *The Sound of Music*, which Louisa had seen more times than she could remember, not that that made any difference to her enjoyment. She sat, misty-eyed, her gentle mouth very slightly open, oblivious of Claudia and Lars holding hands beside her and Simon Savage, sitting well back and watching her face, with no expression on his own features at all. Anyone looking at him might have concluded that he had seen the film too and had gone into a trance until it was over.

When the film was finished the dancing began. The men had surged to the bar, but at the first sound of Abba on the tape, they were back, swinging their partners on to the floor. Louisa, who had watched Lars and Claudia join the cheerful dancing throng, felt a wave of relief when a young giant of a man she had seen several times on the quay advanced upon her with a friendly: 'Yes?' and danced her off too. Only then did she admit to her fear of being left high and dry and Simon

Savage coming to find her without a partner. He would have danced with her, of course, with the frigid politeness of someone doing his duty. . .

The tape came to an end and she was still exchanging small talk with her partner when the music started again, and this time it was Simon Savage who danced her off. A neat dancer, she conceded, and self-assured. After a few minutes she relaxed and began to enjoy herself.

'You are enjoying yourself?' enquired Simon, way up above her head.

'Very much, thank you.'

'It compares not unfavourably with the more sophisticated night spots of London?'

She glanced up briefly. 'I wouldn't know—I've never been to one.'

He didn't answer and she spent several fruitless moments trying to think of something light and amusing to say, but she couldn't—and anyway, Simon was hardly eager for conversation. They danced in silence, and presently, when the tape was changed, they went on dancing, and except for a short spell with Lars and ten minutes of disco dancing with another young man who owned a fishing boat and who had passed the time of day with her on occasion, Simon continued to dance with her for the rest of the evening. He was, she felt, exceeding his duty by doing so, especially as there were several pretty girls there, but it seemed that his duty didn't include talking. Probably he was working out a new bridge.

The evening came to an end. Everyone put on layers of warm clothing and went out into the cold, calling goodnights as they went. Louisa was glad that the distance was short to the house. The idea of facing a trip on the fjord before one got home was rather more than one would wish for at that time of night. She went indoors thankfully and went at once to her room, leaving the others downstairs. It was to be hoped that Simon would have the sense to go to his room too and give the other two a chance to say goodnight before Lars went back to the hotel. She was undressed and in bed, almost asleep, when there was a gentle knock on her door and it was opened.

'You're awake?' It was more a statement than a question, uttered in Simon's voice, surprisingly quiet. He came in, shutting the door behind him, and Louisa sat up in bed and switched on the bedside light.

'Claudia—I heard her come up to bed. . .'

'Where she is now. There's been an accident—a gust of wind overturned one of the launches—three men on board, all saved but in poor shape. They are bringing them in now. Will you come down to the hotel as soon as you can?'

'Give me five minutes.' She barely waited for him to be gone before she was out of bed, tearing off her sensible long-sleeved nightie, bundling into woollies, a sweater, slacks, her jacket, her woolly cap crammed down on to her flowing hair. She crept downstairs in her wool socks and wondered briefly if it was all right to leave Claudia on her own, but there was nothing much she could do about that. She closed the outer door quietly and felt the shock of the bitter wind and cold night as she hurried to the hotel.

The door was shut, but there were lights on downstairs. She opened it and went inside and found that the first of the men was already there, lying on one of the larger tables, covered with a blanket. Two men were bending over him, but they straightened up as she went to look and stood back a little. The man was young and suffering, she judged, from his immersion in the fjord, but his colour wasn't too bad and his pulse was fairly strong. She got the men to help her turn him on to his side, made sure that he had a free air passage, and began to strip off his outer clothes. Someone, she was glad to see, had already taken off his boots and there were plenty of dry blankets piled near. She set the men to rub his arms and legs once his clothes were off, took his pulse again and turned round as the second man was brought in—

an older man this time, and not a good colour.
The four men carrying him laid him on
another blanket-covered table and while she
took a quick look at him, began to take off
his clothes and boots too. Louisa removed
false teeth, took a faint pulse and requested
towels, and when they came set to to rub the
man's legs and arms, presently handing over
to her helpers while she went back to look at
the first man. He was decidedly better and
would be better still for a warm bed and a
good sleep once he was conscious. She
judged him to be safe enough to leave and
went back to the other man.

No one had said very much, doing as she
asked them without query, and now the landlord appeared, his wife behind him, carrying
a tray loaded with mugs and coffee pots and
the potent spirit Aqua Vitae, and hard on their
heels came the third patient, carried carefully
by another four men, Simon Savage being
one of them. He looked across the room as
they laid the man, little more than a boy, on
a table and said briefly: 'I think he has a
broken leg.'

As indeed he had, a nasty compound frac-
ture of the tibia and probably more than that.
Louisa set about covering the ugly jagged
wound, thankful that he was unconscious
still, and then with Simon Savage's help
gently straightened the leg and splinted it.

There might not be a doctor in the small community, but at least they had an excellent first aid equipment. The boy had had a blow on the head as well, there was a discoloration over one eye, but his pulse was good and his pupils were reacting. She finished her work with calm unhurry and said: 'They'll need to go into hospital. The first one is not too bad, but he'll have to have a check-up.'

'Lars and some of the men are getting a launch ready now,' Simon told her. 'We'll take them up to Tromso. You'll come with us.'

Orders, orders! thought Louisa. He could have said please, it would have made a trying situation a little less trying. She said, 'Very well,' and then, 'Claudia is alone.'

'Lars is going up there for the rest of the night. Are we ready to go?'

'Who are "we"?' She was taking pulses again, doing a careful last-minute check.

'You, me, Arne and Knut, the boy you were dancing with.'

Louisa took the coffee the landlord was offering her and took a heartening sip. She wasn't sure, but she thought that he had put Aqua Vitae into it, a good idea if they were to face the cold again. Simon Savage was gulping his down too and then Arne and Knut came in, swallowed their drinks, listened to Simon's instructions, and went away again.

One by one the three men were carried down to the quay, into the launch and made comfortable. Louisa was barely aboard when Simon shouted for a man to cast off, and took the wheel. There was a hard wind blowing within a very few minutes, and Louisa quite understood how the boat the three men had been in had overturned; she only hoped the launch was made of sterner stuff. They lurched and slithered, and if she had had the time she would have indulged in seasickness, but what with keeping the three men on the benches, taking pulses, and when the first man regained consciousness, reassuring him, she had not a moment to spare.

The journey seemed unending and she wondered how the men on deck were faring. Now and then she heard them shouting to each other above the wind, but their voices were cheerful. The boy with the broken leg came to for a moment and she had a job to quieten him before he drowsed off again. His cries brought Simon Savage into the cabin, together with a blast of icy air. 'All right?' he wanted to know. 'We're coming in now. There should be an ambulance waiting—I phoned ahead.'

It took a little while to manoeuvre the three men off the launch and on to the quay, where two ambulances were parked. Louisa, told by Simon to get into the second one, did so, looking round anxiously to see what everyone else was doing—surely they weren't going to leave her here?

'Don't worry,' said Simon laconically. 'Arne and Knut will wait here in the launch for us.' He shut the doors on her and a moment later they moved off.

She was very tired by now and cold to her bones. The hospital, when they reached it, was a blur of bright lights and briskly moving figures. Modern, she thought, escorting the boy into the casualty department, and well equipped. If she hadn't been so worn out she would have been glad to have looked around her. As it was she was told kindly to sit down and waved to one of the benches and someone brought her a cup of coffee. Everyone had disappeared by now. She closed her eyes and dozed, to be roused presently by Simon Savage. 'We're going back,' he told her. 'One of the ambulances will give us a lift to the launch.'

She nodded. 'The men—will they be all right?'

'Yes. You did a good job, Louisa—thanks.'

He bundled her into the ambulance, beside the driver, and got in beside her, then hauled her out again and helped her on to the launch. 'Inside,' he said, and she sat down thankfully on one of the benches and would have gone to sleep again if Knut hadn't come in with more coffee, laced with Aqua Vitae, and stood over her while she drank it. She went to sleep within minutes, which was a good thing, as they were heading into a gale force wind which sent the launch heaving and shuddering and would have terrified her if she had been awake. As it was she had to be shaken when they finally got back.

'Are we there already?' she asked querulously, and tried to go to sleep again, and when she got another shake, 'I must have gone to sleep.'

'You're swimming in spirits,' said Simon. 'We came back in a gale and it seemed best to knock you out.' He hoisted her to her feet. 'Can you manage to walk?'

The cold air revived her and she managed very well, with his arm around her, and at the door she asked: 'What's the time? I seem to have lost track. . .'

He opened the door and pushed her gently inside. 'It's almost five o'clock. Are you hungry?'

She discovered that she was and nodded.

'Go upstairs and get ready for bed and then come down to the kitchen.'

Louisa nodded again and stumbled upstairs and into her room. The sight of her bed almost sent her into it, still dressed as she was, but she had no doubt at all that if she didn't present herself downstairs within a reasonable time, Simon would be wanting to know why not. She undressed and went back to the kitchen, wrapped in the thick dressing gown she had bought for warmth rather than glamour. Certainly there wasn't a vestige of glamour about her. White-faced, her hair in rats' tails, her eyes heavy with sleep, she wandered into the warm little room and found the table laid with plates and mugs and knives and forks. Simon, that most unlikely of cooks, had fried eggs in a pan, made a pot of tea, and cut slices off a brown loaf.

They sat opposite each other hardly speaking, and when they had finished they cleared the table, left everything tidy and went out into the little hall. 'Where will you sleep?' asked Louisa, suddenly remembering that Lars was there.

'It won't be the first time I've slept in a chair.' Indeed, now that she looked closely at him, he looked tired to death.

She said in a motherly voice: 'Oh, poor you! I'll get some blankets and a pillow...'

Simon shook his head. 'Go to bed.' He smiled down at her, a wide, tender smile that made her blink, and then bent his head to kiss her—quick and hard and not at all like the other kiss he had given her. If she hadn't been three parts asleep she would have been filled with astonishment. As it was, she fell into bed aware of a complete contentment, although about what, she had no idea.

CHAPTER EIGHT

IT was Elsa who wakened Louisa later in the morning with a cup of tea and the news that Mr Savage had gone to Tromso to see how the three men were faring, and Miss Savage and Herre Helgesen had gone skiing.

Louisa showered and dressed and went downstairs, had a cup of coffee and a slice of toast in the kitchen and set about laying the table for lunch. Everyone would be back soon; it was almost one o'clock. But one o'clock came and passed and she went into the kitchen to confer with Elsa, who shook her head and said that she really didn't know. Miss Savage had taken a packet of sandwiches with her, but she had said nothing about not coming back at the usual time, and as for Mr Savage, he had said nothing at all, merely walked out of the house—it was Herre Helgesen who had told her where he had gone. Luckily it was a meal which would come to no harm. She looked enquiringly at Louisa because she always went home after she had seen to the midday meal and it was already over her normal time.

Louisa assured her that she could cope

quite easily with the dishing up when the others came home and begged her to take extra time off as she had been so inconvenienced, so Elsa got into her outdoor things, wished her a pleasant Sunday afternoon, and hurried off, leaving Louisa to potter in the kitchen for a while and then go back to sit by the stove, but by now it was almost two o'clock and she was famished, so she went into the kitchen again, helped herself to a plate of Elsa's delicious casserole and ate it at the kitchen table and then, because she was still hungry, she cut a hunk of cheese and ate that before washing her plate and setting the tea tray. Somebody must come back soon, the light was already fading fast into black night. She set the kettle to boil on the wood stove in the sitting room and sat down again to read, but presently she let the book fall and allowed her thoughts to roam.

It seemed likely that she would be going back to England soon. Claudia didn't really need her now; Lars had been the miracle that was needed, if Claudia loved him enough she wouldn't drink again as long as she lived—they would marry and live happily ever after in Bergen. And Simon? Presumably he would go on building bridges wherever they were needed in the world. He was entirely self-sufficient and content with his lot. Presumably he had a home somewhere in

England. He might even marry one day; he would make a terrible husband, she considered, although just once or twice she had glimpsed a quite different man behind that dark austere face. He had been kind to her, too. She remembered his smile and smiled herself, thinking about it. Undoubtedly there was another Simon Savage tucked away somewhere. . .

It was warm in the room and she dozed off, thinking about him still, and awakened to hear Claudia's voice and Lars' deeper tones.

They stopped in surprise when they saw her. 'Have you been here all day?' asked Claudia, and started flinging her jacket and cap and scarf on to chairs and kicking off her boots. 'We thought you'd go with Simon.'

Louisa tried to remember if he'd said anything about taking her out and couldn't— how awful if he had, and she'd gone on sleeping when she should have been up and dressed and ready. 'I didn't wake up,' she said uncertainly.

Claudia shrugged. 'Oh, well, probably he didn't want you, anyway—only he said he was going to the hospital at Tromso, and that's your meat and drink, isn't it?'

Louisa didn't answer but picked up the dropped clothes and asked if they'd like tea. 'There's dinner in the oven,' she explained, 'but it'll keep until you want it.'

They decided to have tea and Lars went into the kitchen to get the tray while Louisa whipped upstairs with Claudia's things. Claudia looked fantastically happy, but she looked tired too.

'Where did you go?' Louisa asked when she got downstairs again.

'Oh, miles and miles—it was heaven,' Claudia answered her carelessly. 'Lars, must you really go back to Bergen?' She smiled at him beguilingly. 'One more day?'

He shook his head. 'No, my dear, I have to go, but I'll come again, as often as I can.'

'Why can't I come with you?' Claudia's voice was dangerously high.

'Because another week or two here is what you need; I want a healthy beautiful girl for a wife and I'm prepared to wait for her.'

Louisa poured tea, feeling *de trop*, and after her first cup she escaped to the kitchen with a muttered excuse which no one listened to, made herself another pot of tea and sat on the table drinking it. She felt incredibly lonely.

When she went back to the sitting room an hour later, the two of them were so absorbed in their talk that she had to ask twice when they wanted their supper.

'We're going over to the hotel,' said Claudia. 'I daresay Simon will be back, and you can eat together.'

'He'll be able to tell you about the men in hospital,' suggested Lars kindly. 'They're all talking about you, you know, saying how splendid you were.'

'Oh, are they? I didn't do anything.' She smiled at them both and went back to the kitchen and stayed there until they left, calling cheerfully that they wouldn't be late back.

'I've got a key,' said Claudia from the door. 'Go to bed if you want to.'

Louisa went back to the sitting room, cleared away the tea things, plumped up the cushions, made up the stove and sat down. If Simon didn't turn up by seven o'clock she was going to have her supper; the casserole was more than ready and she was hungry.

All the same, it was half an hour after that time when she finally had her supper. She ate it on her lap, wondering if the launch had turned turtle on the way back from Tromso. It was more than likely that Simon had gone to a hotel there and had a slap-up meal— probably with some lovely Norwegian lady, she thought gloomily, and then told herself sharply that it didn't matter to her in the least with whom he went out.

By ten o'clock she had had enough. She washed the dishes, tidied the kitchen and went up to bed. It wasn't long after that that she heard Claudia and Lars come in and after a murmur of voices, Claudia came upstairs.

What seemed like hours later, she heard Simon Savage's deliberate footsteps coming into the house. She listened to him making up the stove, going into the kitchen, retracing his steps to his workroom and finally the clink of a glass—whisky; perhaps he was chilled to the marrow, hungry, soaking wet. . . By a great effort she stayed in bed, although every instinct was willing her to go down and warm up the rest of the casserole. It was an hour or more before he came upstairs and it wasn't until then that she allowed herself to go to sleep.

The next day was a bad one. Claudia, without Lars to keep her happy, was at her very worst. She refused to get out of bed, she threw her breakfast tray at Louisa, declared her intention of leaving for Bergen that very morning, swore that she would kill anyone who tried to stop her, and then dissolved into a flood of hysterical tears. Louisa, picking up broken china, was just in time to meet Simon Savage, coming up the stairs like the wrath of God, and order him down again.

'Don't you dare!' she admonished him. 'She's only upset because Lars isn't here— it'll be all right presently. . .' She shooed him step by step until they were back to the hall. 'Go on,' she told him firmly, 'go and build your bridge! You don't understand women, even if you do know how to make a bridge stay up.'

His face, black with temper, suddenly broke into a smile. 'I think you may be right there, Louisa. How fierce you are!' He kissed the end of her nose and turned her round. 'Up you go!'

He was wise enough not to come back until well after tea time, and by then Claudia was at least trying for self-control. A phone call from Lars had helped, of course, and Louisa's patient, uncomplaining company. Halfway through a good wallow in self-pity Claudia paused long enough to observe: 'I don't know how you can put up with me—I'd be gone like a bat out of hell if I'd been you.' But before Louisa could answer that she was in floods of tears again.

Simon behaved beautifully when he did come back home. Bearing an armful of magazines and the newest papers, he put them down beside his stepsister, wished the room at large a good evening, and went into his workroom, where he stayed until Louisa summoned him to supper. And during that meal he talked with unusual placidity about Bergen, Lars' house, his work, his interest in sport, and from there he passed to the various churches in the city, remarking that Lars always went to St Jorgen Church. 'It might be a good place in which to marry,' he suggested mildly, 'because they hold English church services there as well.'

Claudia looked up from the food she was pushing round her plate.

'You don't mind if I marry Lars? You've always disagreed with everything I've wanted to do—hated my friends. . .'

Louisa watched his saturnine features, ready for an outburst. None came. He said mildly: 'Won't you in all fairness agree that I had good reason to dislike them? Do you really want them as friends?' He shrugged. 'Not that it's any business of mine any more, but I'm not sure if Lars will care for them.'

'Oh, I know that—you don't have to preach at me, but I won't want friends now, will I, I've got him.' She got up from the table. 'I'm not hungry. 'I'm going to bed. Louisa, you can bring me up some coffee and a sandwich later.'

'If it were not for the fact that you would scold me severely, I would have made Claudia apologise for talking to you like that,' remarked Simon evenly.

'She doesn't mean it—she's unhappy. . .' Louisa gave him the briefest of glances, wishing to appear matter-of-fact after their meeting that morning.

'And you? Are you happy?'

'Yes. You see, Claudia is almost cured, isn't she? Oh, I know she's had relapses before, but this time there's Lars. I think he loves her so much that he's prepared to put up with a good deal.'

'And would you like to be loved like that, Louisa?'

'Yes, of course I should, but it doesn't happen to everyone, does it?'

He didn't reply, but presently said: 'I had planned to take you both to Tromso for a day's shopping, but the weather forecast is bad and it's too risky.'

'Perhaps in a few days—it would do Claudia a lot of good. How are the three men?'

'In good shape; two of them will be coming back in a few days, the boy will have to stay for a bit, but he's got relatives in Tromso, so it won't be too bad for him.' He was staring at her steadily. 'Everyone here is proud of you, do you know that?'

She looked down at her empty plate and could think of nothing to say. Presently she broke a silence which had gone on for too long. 'Mr Savage. . .'

'And that's another thing—why am I always Mr Savage? We have Lars and Arne and Knut and Mr Savage, as though I were some mid-Victorian ogre. My name is Simon.'

She poured herself more coffee which she didn't want, but it gave her something to do.

She said very quietly: 'But you were an ogre,' and heard his sigh, and the next moment he had got to his feet.

'Well, I've some work to do,' he was icily bland. 'Goodnight.'

She didn't see him again until the following evening and by then she was tired and a little cross. Claudia had been very trying, although there were signs that she was pulling herself together again. After all, Lars had promised to come up for the following weekend. Louisa reminded her of this at frequent intervals and talked herself hoarse about the new clothes Claudia insisted she must have. 'I shall want a great deal of money, heaps of it,' she declared. 'Simon will just have to foot the bills. I'm not getting married without a rag to my back!' An inaccurate statement Louisa ignored, only too happy to get Claudia in a more cheerful frame of mind. She wasn't quite as happy when Claudia brought the matter up at the supper table. The conversation between the three of them had been a little forced and Simon looked tired and bad-tempered too. But to her surprise he agreed placidly that Claudia should have enough money to buy what she needed. He even suggested that she might like to fly to Oslo and shop there.

'Does that mean that we can get away from here soon?' Claudia demanded.

'Very soon now—it's up to you, Claudia.'

'I'm on the waggon,' she promised him. 'I swore to Lars that I'll not drink another drop, and I won't—you see, I don't need to. What about Louisa?'

His glance flickered over her before he answered his stepsister.

'I think we might dispose with Louisa's services very shortly,' he said casually. Just as though I'm not sitting here, thought Louisa indignantly, and quelled the temptation to ask when she was to go. Let him tell her, she couldn't care less. She just stopped herself in time from tossing her head.

She didn't have long to wait. 'How about the end of the week?' he asked smoothly. 'Lars is coming up for the weekend, isn't he? I shall be finished here in four or five days. I don't see why you and Lars shouldn't go back together, and we can put Louisa on a flight the day before that.'

'To London?' asked Claudia without much interest.

'Where else?' Again that quick glance.

She conjured up a smile and said brightly: 'Oh, how lovely, home for Christmas!'

The very thought appalled her. She would have to find another job before that—go to an agency and take anything, preferably something that kept her so busy she wouldn't have a moment to remember Norway and

Claudia or, for that matter, Simon Savage.

Now that plans were made and Claudia felt secure in a happy future, she shed her bad habits like some old outworn skin. For the next two days she got up for breakfast, insisted on taking Louisa on to the slope to teach her more about skiing, made her own bed and spent barely an hour on her face and hair. Louisa could hardly believe that this was the same woman who had engaged her in London, the change was so great. Of course, Claudia still took little interest in anyone else but herself and Lars. Beyond supposing that Louisa would get herself another job quickly she didn't mention her going and even remarked that it would be delightful to be on her own—at least until she married, she added quickly. 'You're not a bad kid,' she told Louisa, 'but it's like having a ball and chain attached to me, but I suppose you have to put up with that if you're a nurse—a necessary evil, aren't you?' She had laughed and Louisa had laughed with her. No one had ever called her that before, it gave her a nasty cold feeling in her insides, but she would have died rather than let Claudia see how shattered she felt.

And Simon made it much worse that evening, talking at great length and with remarkable fluency for him about the delights of the Norwegian Christmas. 'Everything shuts down at midday on Christmas Eve,' he informed her, 'and there's a traditional dish of dried lamb served in the evening and afterwards everyone gathers round the Christmas tree and sings carols before the presents. Christmas Day is much the same and on the next day—our Boxing Day—they give enormous parties with skiing and sleigh rides and masses of food.' He fixed Louisa with his dark eyes. 'You would have enjoyed it, Louisa.'

She gave him a cross look. Of course she would have enjoyed it, the idea of going back to England didn't appeal to her at all, but what else could she do? They had made it plain enough that she was no longer needed—they would probably be relieved to see her go. She toyed with the idea of staying in Bergen. Christmas wasn't so far off and if she was careful, she would have enough money. There had been little or no chance to spend much, but if she did Claudia might think that she was staying deliberately in order to spy on her. Besides, she had made it plain that she would be glad to see her go. She said woodenly: 'I'm sure I should, it sounds delightful.' And as she said it she was struck by the sudden knowledge that that was what she wanted more than anything in the world—to stay in Norway for Christmas, for ever, if necessary, just as long as she could be with Simon Savage. Falling in love with him had been the last thing she had expected to do. He was ill-tempered, brusque, impatient and intolerant. He was also, she now perceived, the only man she wanted to marry.

'How utterly silly!' she muttered, and earned a surprised look from him. She said the first thing which entered her head: 'Do I fly direct to England or must I change planes?'

'Tromso to Bergen and Bergen to Heathrow.'

'How nice,' she observed idiotically, and waffled on about the journey, the delights of Christmas at home, seeing her friends again, so intent on painting a carefree picture of her future that she quite missed Simon's puzzled look which presently turned to speculation.

And if she had hoped, during her wakeful night, for some small sign that he might want to meet her again at some time, she was disappointed. He was more austere than usual over the breakfast table, telling Claudia in a forthright manner that on no account were they to go skiing that day. 'There's bad weather coming,' he assured her, 'probably there'll be no flights to Tromso. . .'

'Then Lars won't be able to come?'

'Probably not.'

She shot him a furious look. 'Then I shall go to him.'

'No, if you get to Tromso and the planes are grounded there, you might not be able to get back here. I suggest that you ring him during the morning.' He had gone before she could answer and Louisa was forced to listen to recriminations for the next ten minutes or so; not that she listened very hard, for her head was full of her own problems.

Lars telephoned during the morning. There were violent snowstorms in the south of the country and all flights had been cancelled and he would come just as soon as he could—a statement which met with an outburst of tears on Claudia's part and an hysterical request to be taken to Bergen at once. Even Lars' promise that if the weather delayed him for too long he would travel by the coastal steamer did little to cheer her up. He rang off finally and Claudia went up to her room and locked the door.

It was getting on for midday when she came downstairs again, and daylight, which would last a mere two hours or so, had come. The sky was blue and there wasn't a cloud to be seen from the window and she pointed this out to Louisa. 'They've slipped up,' she said hopefully. 'There's not a sign of snow.'

Louisa glanced out at the sky. 'We can't see a great deal from here,' she pointed out.

'Would you like me to start your packing?'

Claudia sprawled in a chair and picked up a book. 'After lunch—would you go to the shop for me? There are several things I simply must have—I'll make a list while you get your jacket.'

It was quite a long list and Louisa read it with surprise. 'But you can get most of these in Bergen. I mean, none of them are urgent. . .'

Claudia barely glanced up from her reading. 'Don't argue. I want them now—unless you're too lazy to go and get them?'

Louisa bit back an angry retort and went out of the house without a word. What did it matter, she asked herself tiredly; what did anything matter?

It took her fifteen minutes to do the shopping by the time she had waited her turn, waited while the various odds and ends were found and then had a short chat with Arne's sister. As she started back again, she could see that the fjord's waters were dark and heaving sluggishly and that the blue sky had become less vivid. Perhaps there was bad weather coming after all. She went into the house and straight into the sitting room. Claudia wasn't there, so she picked up her basket and went along to the kitchen. Elsa was standing by the table, getting the lunch and looking put out.

'I am glad you are here,' she began. 'Miss Savage has gone out and there is bad weather coming fast. She would not listen to me. She has taken her skis too. I think that Mr Savage should be told, for she will be lost once the snow comes.'

Louisa dumped her basket on the table. 'Did she say where she was going?' and when Elsa shook her head: 'How long ago?'

'Ten minutes, perhaps.'

'Then I'll try and catch her up and get her to come back. Make me some coffee, Elsa, and put it in a thermos, and I want a torch, and then telephone Mr Savage.' Louisa was searching around for the rucksack which hung in the kitchen and when she had it, rammed in some slices of bread Elsa had just cut and a slab of chocolate and a ball of string she saw on the dresser. She hadn't a very good idea of what one took on such a trip and probably there would be no need to use any of them, all the same she added the coffee and the torch. It had all taken a few precious minutes and Claudia might be miles away by now. She put on the rucksack, urged Elsa to telephone without delay, collected her skis from the back door and hurried through the snow, past the last of the houses, where she put on her skis and started cautiously up the slope where they usually went. Claudia had gone that way; she could see the ski marks very plainly. Once she got to the top she would be able to see in all directions.

It was an interminable time before she got there and in her haste she fell down twice and getting on to her feet again took all her patience and strength, but once there, she stood, fetching her breath, scanning the scene before her. The mountains stretched for miles, snow-covered, terrifying in their grandeur, but far more terrifying was the great bank of cloud, yellow at the edges, devouring the blue sky, and the first hint of the bitter wind hurrying it along at a furious pace. But it wouldn't help to study the sky. She lifted her goggles and surveyed the slopes ahead of her. It took her a minute to spot Claudia, who had skied down the reverse side of the slope and was just beginning to work her way up on the farther side. She was following the route she and Lars had taken together, Louisa guessed. There was a narrow valley which would take her back towards the fjord. Louisa trembled at the thought of the journey ahead of her; she had never ventured farther than the spot she was on at that moment and she was frankly scared. But the longer she stood there, the more terrified she would be. She let out a ringing shout in the hope that Claudia would hear her and for a moment the distant figure paused, but then went on again. Louisa put her goggles back on, took one despairing look at the clouds racing towards her, and set off.

Surprisingly it wasn't as bad as she had expected. The slope was longer than the one she had practised on but no steeper. She reached the bottom, still scared to death but rather pleased with herself too, and started the laborious climb up the other side. Claudia had disappeared over the ridge and heaven knew what nightmares waited on the other side. A few paper-dry snowflakes began to fall and Louisa, by a great effort, kept her pace deliberate. Hurrying would mean another spill and she hadn't the time to waste. By the time she reached the top the snow was falling in earnest and it was getting ominously dark. She stood at the top, gasping for breath, and looked around her. There wasn't much to see now, for there was a thick curtain of snow and the wind had gathered a ferocious strength. She gazed around helplessly. Claudia's ski tracks had already been covered by the snow, and there was no way of knowing which way she had gone. She wiped her goggles, turned her back to the wind and shouted with all her might.

There was an answering shout, very faint; impossible to tell from where it came. She couldn't see the lower slopes ahead of her. Suppose she skied to the bottom, passed Claudia and had to come back? She would lose her way and make matters worse. She said out loud: 'Oh, God, please give a hand,' and just for a few seconds the wind dropped and the snow thinned, and away to her left, half way down, she saw a small dark object.

'Oh, thanks very much,' said Louisa fervently, and plunged downwards at an angle, going very carefully. She hadn't learned to turn on skis yet and she hoped she had got the direction right.

She had, she was on top of Claudia before she could stop herself, and they both fell in a mêlée of arms and legs and skis. Claudia was up first and pulled Louisa to her feet. She said bitterly: 'I've been all kinds of a fool—I'm sorry, Louisa,' which was the first time she had ever apologised to her. And probably the last, thought Louisa, busy brushing snow off herself.

'We'll have to make some sort of shelter,' she shouted above the wind. 'I asked Elsa to ring Simon, they'll be out looking for us by now, but we'll freeze if we stay here.'

Claudia clutched at her arm. 'There's a hut somewhere close—we passed it when we came this way, Lars and I. It's somewhere to the left, on an outcrop of rock, it's got a turf roof.'

Louisa remembered the string in her rucksack. 'Let's find it,' she shouted back, 'but we'd better tie ourselves together.' She turned her back. 'In the rucksack.'

It was a botched-up job, what with thick mitts they dared not take off and granny knots which didn't stay done up, but in the end they achieved a double line of string fastening them together. It would certainly snap if one of them fell, but it was better than nothing at all. The snow was falling so thickly now that they couldn't see more than a few feet in front of them; but through the gloom it was still possible to make out the outline of the mountains whenever the wind dropped and the snow stopped swirling around them. Claudia remembered that the hut was on the lower slope of a mountain with a peak which towered above the rest. They had to wait a little while before she could locate it and even when they did they weren't sure that they weren't skiing in circles. When they at last saw the hut in front of their noses after several false starts they were ready to cry with fright and relief and tiredness—indeed, Claudia did burst into tears, and Louisa, on the verge of snivelling herself, told her sharply to stop at once. 'Unless you want to die of cold,' she said. 'Get inside, do—I've got coffee with me and some bread and chocolate and we'll do exercises to keep warm.'

'No one will ever find us,' wailed Claudia.

'Simon will,' declared Louisa stoutly. 'I'm going to shine my torch presently.' She had pushed Claudia into the tiny place and turned to look round at their surroundings. It was a very small hut but stoutly built, with no windows and an open small door, but at least it was shelter. She took off her rucksack, opened the coffee and gave some to Claudia, had some herself and then shared the food, and when they had devoured the last crumb she made Claudia jump up and down and wave her arms. It was difficult, the two of them in the tiny place, floundering about, bumping into each other, but she kept Claudia at it until they were both exhausted even though they were less frozen. Claudia sat down on the rucksack and declared that she had to rest even if she froze solid, and Louisa let her, for the time being at least.

'Why did you do it?' she asked.

'Oh, I don't know——I suppose I was disappointed and upset, and I don't take kindly to not getting my own way, and I've always made a point of doing the opposite of whatever Simon has told me to do.' Claudia gave a choked laugh. 'If we ever get out of this I'll be a reformed character!' She glanced at Louisa. 'Why did you come after me?'

'I'm still in Simon's employ.' The thought of him made her want to cry. She said matter-of-factly: 'I'm going to have a try with the torch. What's the time?'

'Just after two o'clock.'

It seemed a lot longer than the two hours since she had started out from the house. Surely a search party would be out looking for them by now? She put her head cautiously round the edge of the door and saw that for the moment the snow had lessened, although the wind was still blowing hard. The thought of the journey back, if ever they were lucky enough to make it, made her feel sick.

It was a pity that she never could remember SOS in Morse, but surely any kind of light in such a desolate spot would attract attention—if only it could be seen. And she had lost her sense of direction, too, which meant sending a beam to all points of the compass. Nothing happened; she repeated her flashes several times and then went to crouch inside again. Claudia had gone to sleep and Louisa wasn't sure if this was a good thing or not. She decided not to wake her for half an hour and got down beside her on the iron hard floor, holding her close so that they might share each other's warmth.

The half hour went slowly. At the end of it she got up again, wakened an unwilling Claudia and after five minutes waving their arms and stamping their feet, she poked her head out once more. It seemed to her that the appalling weather wasn't quite so appalling as it had been. She had no idea how long such storms lasted and as the daylight hours had already passed, it was too dark to see any possible landmarks, but she was sure that the snow was lessening. She flashed her torch and peered hopefully for a reply, and when there wasn't one, flashed it again. Nothing happened. She would wait ten minutes and then try again. She took one last look and turned round to scan the gloom behind her—and saw a light.

The torch was still in her hand; excitement made her drop it. She searched for it frantically, quite forgetting to shout. She had to have the torch; whoever it was might miss them and they would die of cold and hunger. She was still grovelling round, sniffing and sobbing under her breath, when someone swished to a halt within inches of her, plucked her off the ground and wrapped her so close that she had no breath.

'So there you are,' said Simon, and kissed her cold face hard and still with one arm round her, turned the torch slung round his neck so that it shone behind him. 'The others will be here in a minute. Where's Claudia?'

'Inside.'

He pushed her back into the hut and followed. He spoke gently to Claudia, who was in floods of tears, and only grunted when she paused long enough to say: 'You took long enough—I could have died, and I won't go back until the snow stops.'

Simon had coffee with him. He shared it between them and they had barely finished it when men began crowding into the small place, cheerful men who declared that the weather was improving, offering more coffee, handing out sandwiches, making much of them. Arne, who had crouched beside Louisa, said kindly: 'You see that now you are a good skier—you will no longer be afraid.'

She smiled back at him. 'Oh, but I shall! I'm a complete coward, and I'm so sorry that we—we got lost; that you all had to come and look for us, and in this appalling weather.'

She didn't know that Simon was behind her. She spilt her coffee when he said quietly: 'You have no need to apologise, Louisa, it was very brave of you to follow Claudia, who should have known better. My God, what a trouble that woman has been to me, and how glad I am that Lars is fool enough to take her on for the rest of his life.'

'They'll be very happy,' Louisa mumbled.

They had two sledges with them. Claudia was wrapped up and strapped into one of them, but Louisa absolutely refused to travel on the other. 'I'll manage very well,' she declared firmly. 'It's the last chance I'll have of skiing before I leave and I don't want to miss it.'

They travelled in two files and Simon

stayed with her the whole way, and when she fell over, which she did several times, he picked her up, dusted her down, and urged her on again, almost without speaking. She had never been so happy in her life before. The snow and wind were suddenly wonderful, the mountains not terrifying at all; she could ski and Mr Savage had turned into Simon at last. She closed her eyes, remembering his kiss, and fell over once more. They were almost home by then. Heaven, she felt sure, was just round the corner.

CHAPTER NINE

BUT heaven was rather further away than Louisa had thought. There was a good deal of bustle and confusion once they were back at home. Claudia demanded a great deal of attention, declaring that she felt faint, that she must have a hot bath at once, that she needed food, that she must telephone Lars immediately. She had thanked the men perfunctorily before she had gone upstairs, and it was left to Louisa and Elsa to hand round coffee and pastries and thank them more warmly. And Simon, when she looked for him, had disappeared. She shook hands with their rescuers and when the last of them had gone, went slowly upstairs to Claudia, who was calling for her.

'Where have you been?' she asked impatiently. 'I want you to rub in that cream for me—my skin will be ruined. Lord, I'm tired!'

'And so am I,' observed Louisa shortly, making quick work of the creaming and bustling Claudia into bed without giving her a chance to think of anything else she wanted done. 'Elsa's staying late, she'll bring you

up your supper presently. I'm going to have
a bath.'

She was still in it daydreaming about
Simon when he came back into the house.
He didn't stay long; Elsa told him that his
stepsister was in bed and she thought Louisa
was going to bed too. He thanked her quietly
and went to the hotel and had a meal there—
which was a pity, because presently Louisa
went downstairs, looking a little wan, but
nicely made up and wearing one of her
Norwegian sweaters and a thick skirt, all
ready to have her supper with Simon. But the
table, she saw at once, was laid for one and
when she asked, Elsa told her that Mr Savage
had only called in for a moment to see if they
were all right before going to the hotel.

And although she was tired and remarkably sleepy by now, Louisa waited patiently
until Elsa had gone home and the clock struck
the hour of ten. But Simon didn't come. If
he had wanted to he would have been back
by now—and what a good thing, she told
herself, for she would have made a fool of
herself if he had. It was time she learnt that
kisses could mean nothing. She had no doubt
that when they met in the morning he would
be Mr Savage once more.

She was right. She went down to breakfast
alone, because Claudia was certain that she
was going to have a cold, and found him

already at table eating the heavenly porridge Elsa made so beautifully. He wished her good morning, barely glancing at her and enquiring after Claudia.

'She thinks she's caught a cold,' said Louisa.

'Impossible. The one thing you can't get in these parts is the common cold.' He spoke coldly, very sure of himself, and she gave his bowed head a loving look, suddenly conscious of the fact that tomorrow she would be having breakfast with him for the last time. She put down her spoon, quite unable to eat, and he said at once: 'What's the matter? Aren't you well?'

He sounded so impatient that she picked up her spoon again and made herself finish the bowlful. 'I've never felt better,' she told him. 'I'm getting excited about going home.'

He put down the paper he was studying. 'I find that hard to believe,' he observed evenly. 'You don't like your home—besides, you kissed me very thoroughly yesterday.'

She went very red but met his eyes frankly. 'I was very glad to see you—I thought we were going to die. I—I got carried away.'

'Ah, you kissed me in fact under great provocation.'

'I—well, yes, that's about it. I'm sorry, I expect people do silly things when they're a bit upset.'

Simon lowered his eyes to the paper. 'And not only when they're upset,' he observed.

And that was the sum total of their conversation. Louisa did have a try just once. She began: 'I do want to thank you. . .'

His laconic 'Don't' stopped her more effectively than anything else could have done.

The storm had blown itself out. There was a great deal more snow, and the waters of the fjord carried small chunks of ice on its steely grey surface, but the sky was clear. There would be more storms, of course, but planes and helicopters were flying again, Lars would be coming to fetch his Claudia back to Bergen and Louisa would leave as had been arranged. No one had given her a ticket yet, although Simon had mentioned casually that he had it. She took Claudia's breakfast upstairs, finished the last of her packing, and put on her outdoor things. There was nothing more for her to do until she left in the morning and her room, shorn of her small possessions, looked uninviting. The sky was clear and the brief day wasn't far off. The little huddle of houses, painted in their cheerful blues and pinks and greens, gleamed in the street lamps' bright beams and the snow reflected them, so that one hardly noticed the darkness. The shop was full and she went inside to say goodbye and then on to the quay to speak to

Arne and several of the other men who had
become her friends.

She stayed talking for a few minutes and
then struggled through the snow to the curve
of the fjord to get a last look at the bridge. It
was finished, they had told her, and was to
be opened very shortly. Men were busy there
now, packing up the scaffolding and piling it
tidily at either end. When spring came, it
would be taken away and the little wooden
huts where they had worked during the winter
months would go too. It was a beautiful
bridge, curving gracefully across the grey
water. Louisa turned away wanting to cry,
then made her way back to the hotel, where
she had coffee and a long talk with the owner.

The afternoon dragged. There was no sign
of Simon and Claudia had elected to stay in
bed, exclaiming crossly that of course she
had a cold and what did Simon know about
it anyway. Louisa sat by the stove and tried
to make up her mind what she would do. She
had plenty of friends, but she had no intention
of wishing herself upon them at no notice at
all. And she couldn't face her stepmother—
she didn't give Frank a thought. Somehow
he had slid away into a past which wasn't
important any more.

She had a solitary tea and went on sitting
there, sad and forlorn and quite unable to be
anything else. Elsa went presently and she

took Claudia up the supper she had asked for and then laid the table for two.

Simon didn't come. Louisa ate her meal with a book propped up before her, staring at the same page without reading it, and presently went to bed. She hadn't expected to sleep, but she did, to wake heavy-eyed when her alarm went at seven o'clock. She was almost glad that she would be going within an hour or so; to get it over quickly was all she wanted. She showered and dressed and packed her overnight bag, then went downstairs.

Simon was at the kitchen table eating his breakfast and she sat down opposite him and began on the porridge Elsa put before her. He had said nothing beyond 'Good morning', but there was an envelope beside her plate. She looked at it and then at him and he said shortly: 'Your salary, Louisa,' and added after a tiny pause: 'Thank you for all the care and attention you've given Claudia. It must have been tiresome for you. I hope you'll find something—someone more congenial for your next patient.'

She glanced at him, her eyes very large and soft. She would have liked to have said something suitable in reply, but her throat had closed over. To her horror she felt tears pricking her eyelids and she pushed back her chair and got up. 'Simon,' she whispered

without realising that she had said it.
'Simon. . .' She swallowed the lump in her
throat and said in a breathy little voice: 'I'm
not hungry. I must finish my packing.'

She went to her room and sat on her bed,
and presently Elsa appeared without a word
and put a tray of coffee down on the dressing
table and went away again. Louisa drank all
the coffee, tidied up her face, put on her outdoor things and went to say goodbye to
Claudia.

'Going?' Claudia was only half awake and
not best pleased at being disturbed. 'Oh, well,
goodbye—we're not likely to see each other
again, are we?' She added grudgingly: 'Of
course if you should ever come to Bergen
you must come and see us.' She rolled over
and closed her eyes, and Louisa went and
fetched her bag and went downstairs. The
launch was leaving at eight o'clock and there
was only five minutes left.

Elsa was in her outdoor clothes too and
when Louisa started to say goodbye she said:
'I'm coming to see you off, Louisa,' and they
walked down to the quay together with never
a sight of Simon. Louisa gave Elsa a hug,
shook hands once again with the little crowd
who had come to see her off, and was helped
into the launch—and there was Simon,
longer and leaner than ever, standing on the
deck talking to Arne. He nodded when he

saw her and the people on the quay shouted and waved as the launch slowly crept away from them, out into the fjord. She stood waving until they were distant spots under the bright lights of the little quay and then went into the cabin. She hadn't expected Simon to be there—indeed, she hadn't been thinking rationally at all, for she still had no ticket. She hadn't opened the envelope either. Presently she would do so, and ask about her ticket too, but just for a moment she wanted to sit still and pull herself together. It would never do to let him see that her heart was breaking. He came into the cabin presently, taking up most of the space, and she asked him in a composed voice if she might have her ticket.

'All in good time,' he told her. 'Are you warm enough?'

'Yes, thank you.' Then she asked, 'Are you going to Tromso too?' and blushed at the silliness of the question, but she was answered without a flicker of amusement:

'Well, yes, I am.' And then: 'Don't come on deck, it's very cold.' He went again as silently as he had come.

The journey seemed so short, but only because she wanted it to last for ever. She could see the lights of Tromso as they sped round the last bend; in another five minutes they would be there. She had no idea where the airport was and she didn't much care. She supposed there would be a taxi for her. She wouldn't want to wait around, saying good-bye would be bad enough however quick it was.

Simon came back into the cabin, bringing a gust of icy air with him. 'Ready?' he asked, and picked up her bag.

They had berthed when she went outside and there was a Land Rover parked on the quay. She shook hands with Arne and the boy with him and stepped on to the hard-packed snow, to be joined almost at once by Simon.

'We're going in the Land Rover,' he told her, and when she stared up at him question-ingly: 'I'm flying to Bergen—in fact I'm flying to Heathrow with you.' He put her bag down and pulled her close. 'I didn't dare tell you,' and at her look of astonishment: 'You see, when we met I thought, ''There's a brown mouse of a girl with a sharp tongue,'' and then before I knew what was happening I was in love with you. Oh, I did my best to ignore it, and I thought that if I ignored you too I'd be safely back in my bachelor state in no time—only it didn't work out like that. You were under my skin, in my bones, my very heartbeat. And I'd gone out of my way to make you dislike me so that it would be easier for me to get over you. Only I haven't done that, my darling.' He stared down at her, unsmiling, even a little grim. 'I've discovered that I can't face life without you, indeed I doubt if I could build another bridge. You had a wretched life with Claudia—if only you could bear to take me on instead. . .' A snowflake fell on to her nose and he paused and brushed it off very gently. 'My dearest little Louisa, if only you'd marry me!'

It was bitingly cold and a few snowflakes followed the first one, but Louisa hadn't noticed. She wasn't aware of the men on the launch watching them, or the driver of the Land Rover, for that matter. She had never felt so happy or so warm in her life before.

'Oh, dear Simon, of course I will! I love you too; I never want to leave you.'

He kissed her then, long and hard and with so much warmth that she wondered in a dreamlike way how she could ever have considered him austere and cold. He was most satisfyingly not either of those things. She kissed him back and then leaned back a little in his arms. 'It's a funny place to have a proposal,' she added shakily.

He smiled at her. 'I suppose it is.' He looked round and caught Arne's interested eye and shouted something to him which sent him and the boy as well as the driver hurrying over to them to pump their arms and utter congratulations before they finally got into the Land Rover.

Louisa sat with her hand in Simon's and at the airport she went through reception and Customs and boarded the plane without taking any note at all of her surroundings. She tucked her hand in his again as they were airborne, drank the coffee that was brought round, ate the sandwich she was given like an obedient child, and then went to sleep, her head on his shoulder. And at Bergen there was only a brief wait before they were on the flight to Heathrow. She ate lunch this time, far too excited and happy to have much appetite. They didn't talk much, only as they started the descent to the airport she asked: 'Where are we going?'

'Home,' said Simon, 'to Wiltshire. Shall we be married there and go back to Norway for our honeymoon?'

'Oh, yes, please!' She was still too excited to bother about the details—besides, Simon was there to see to everything. She heaved a sigh of pure happiness and went to sleep again.

There was a car waiting for them when they let Heathrow—a Daimler Sovereign. As Louisa settled into the seat beside Simon she asked: 'How did it get here—this car? Is it yours?'

He nodded. 'When I go abroad I garage it close by and they bring it here for me— it's convenient.' He dropped a kiss on her cheek. 'Not long now, love. About two hours' drive.'

They drove down the M3, through a rain-sodden landscape, strangely green after the snow and the mountains, and then took the road to Warminster, but before they reached it Simon turned off the road, down a country lane which wandered up and down the gentle hills until it reached a very small village. It had a church in its centre and a cluster of houses and cottages round it and standing well back, taking up all of one side of the square, a splendid Queen Anne house with large square windows and a beautiful front door with a fanlight over it and a white-painted porch. Simon drove through the open gate at the side of the narrow front garden and stopped the car.

'Home,' he said, undid her safety belt and leaned across to open the door for her and then got out himself. By the time they had reached the door it was open with a plump smiling woman on the porch, beaming a welcome at them.

'Mrs Turner, my housekeeper.' He corrected himself: '*Our* housekeeper. Mrs Turner, this is my future wife, Miss Louisa Evans.' He waited while they shook hands and then swept Louisa across the hall and into a small room, lined with bookshelves, its great desk covered with maps and papers.

He took Louisa in his arms and pulled the cap off her head.

'This is where I start my bridges,' he said very quietly, 'and this is where our heaven starts, my darling.'

Louisa put up her face to be kissed. 'I thought it would be just round the corner, and it was,' she told him. She would have explained further, but there seemed no point. To be kissed was far more satisfactory.

BETTY NEELS

If you have missed any of the previously published titles in
the Betty Neels Collector's Edition, you may order them by
sending a cheque or postal order (please do not send cash)
made payable to Harlequin Mills & Boon Ltd. for £2.99 per
book plus 50p postage and packing for the first book and
25p for each additional book. Please send your order to:
Betty Neels Collector's Edition, P.O. Box 236, Croydon,
Surrey, CR9 3RU (EIRE: Betty Neels Collector's Edition, P. O.
Box 4546, Dublin 24).

MILLS & BOON®

Medical Romance™

Stories full of tears and joy...
Stories full of love and laughter...
Stories that will touch your heart.

Mills & Boon Medical Romances offer
modern dramas featuring fascinating
characters and emotionally rich relationships
where doctors and nurses battle to save
lives and find everlasting love.

Love is the best medicine of all!

Available wherever Mills & Boon books are sold